Daniel's Obsession

Monica Collins

Copyright © 2021 C. J. Morris
All cover art copyright © 2021 C. J. Morris
All Rights Reserved

This is a work of fiction. Names, places, characters and incidents are either the product of the author's imagination or are used fictitiously, and any resemblance to any actual persons, living or dead, businesses, organizations, events or locales is entirely coincidental.

No part of this book may be reproduced or transmitted in any form or by any means, electronic or mechanical, including photocopying, recording, or by any information storage and retrieval system, without permission in writing from the author.

Publishing Coordinator – Sharon Kizziah-Holmes

Paperback-Press
an imprint of A & S Publishing
A & S Holmes, Inc.

ISBN -13: 978-1-951772-82-6

Acknowledgments

I would like to extend a special thank you to David Kendall, Shauna Evans, Linda Hull, John and Terri Morris, and Allyn Collins, without whom none of this would be possible, for all of their feedback and suggestions in the writing of this novel.

We all want to be loved,

but the world has no plan

for finding our lovers.

PART I

CHAPTER ONE

Daniel King milled about the giant university parking lot nestled between two dormitories, now filled with a circle of floats ready for tomorrow's homecoming parade. Daniel was ready to enjoy the evening's festivities, then get to bed early for tomorrow's game. At 6'1", lean and strong, Daniel played linebacker, a two-year starter. and second on the team in tackles. Off the field, Daniel was a laid-back, easy going, patient listener. He had the clean, fresh face of a twenty-two-year-old and brilliant blue eyes. Because of his easy smile and friendly nature some thought him naive. He did have the inclination to attribute his own feelings as the same as others around him. His good nature did leave him perplexed, at times, when he misread the situation.

A four-foot-high stage had been built in the center of the parking lot. The Atherton University student body rose in a chorus of voices as the lead cheerleader led the throng in the school song. Tomorrow's game would be played against cross-town rival MacArthur State. However, no one could know, before the evening was over, five people currently in attendance would be dead.

A stage, draped with blue and white streamers, filled the center of the lot surrounded by the floats. The supports and floor of the stage had been built from old planking from a dock at the lake. The boards had endured years of being underwater to being high and dry depending upon lake levels. The wood, now as dry as kindling, was ready to split into a million splinters like shards of broken glass. As evening fell into darkness, endless shots from Roman candles climbed into the sky. Other students lit sparklers and fired bottle rockets.

Daniel knew the festivities were more than a pep rally. Opponent MacArthur State University had suffered humiliation far beyond any defeat on the gridiron. Their mascot, the head of a bison, had been stolen from their athletic facility. The thieves escaped undetected. By now, everyone from Atherton U., including professors and administrators, knew of the theft. The homecoming festivities had only begun.

There was no doubt who had pilfered the dried-out buffalo head–athletes from Atherton U. Students at MacArthur were outraged. Atherton University would pay. The Wildcat mascot mounted on a pedestal in front of the Atherton student union was in jeopardy.

Yet, the mascot rivalry before football homecoming was a time-honored tradition between the two schools. Efforts to steal the other school's mascot was a calling card for the bold and daring, but never before had a clean getaway been achieved. In a joyous moment, the Atherton University athletic director held the bison head mounted on a board high above his head. Atherton students loved it. A marching tune blared through the stage speakers.

But in the distance, amidst the throng of cheers and music, Daniel heard a siren. The wail came nearer. An incessant clanking bell accompanied the siren. Within minutes, a 1950's fire engine, refurbished and repaired, turned the corner and sped down the avenue beside the Atherton rally. The driver laid on the horn to add to the discordant noise and a small army of screaming MacArthur students hurled small bags of sand at the Atherton floats.

Retaliation was immediate. Atherton students ran to the edge of the street with their Roman candles and buzz bombs. The fire engine stopped at the end of the block. It hesitated at the corner, backed up, and faced the way it came. The driver gunned the engine. He let his foot off the brake and floored the old machine into the gauntlet of battle-ready Atherton students. At a top speed of 35 miles an hour and headlights ablaze, the engine barreled down the street.

Without the slightest thought to the hazard each side poised to each other, the battle was about to be joined. School pride must be defended. All was intended as a friendly battle against a cross town rival, yet afterward, no one knew exactly what happened. And yet, no one in attendance would forget a second of it for the rest of their lives.

A barrage of fireworks arched toward the red truck. Most sparks fell short or flew over. The driver weaved back and forth across the road to avoid the pyrotechnic onslaught. But a shower of flaming hot Roman candles hit the truck. One hit the driver in the chest in the open-air cab. His shirt burst into flames. Instead of hitting the brake, the driver hit the gas. The fire engine veered straight into the parking lot of the Atherton University rally.

The engine jumped the curb, hit the edge of a float, and roared ahead straight at the stage. No one had time to flinch. A sickening crunch split the air as splintering timbers snapped. Those on stage were blasted twenty feet into the air. Cries of terror and pain followed the devastation, and all the while, the high-pitched siren continued to scream at the moon as the injured and dying moaned about.

The engine slammed through the stage sending deadly debris flying across the lot. A fire began when the engine came to rest. The flames injured no one, but the devastation left in the path of the engine was horror to behold.

Like hundreds of others, Daniel dashed for the grass when the fire engine surged into the lot. He was dazed. He saw, but did he see what he just saw? His pants were torn at the right knee. Everyone ran to those injured. Daniel stood and looked about at the carnage. He ran to one girl knocked to the asphalt by the stampeding crowd. He helped her up. She was frightened, but not hurt and she walked away. He helped others up who had hit the ground trying to avoid the fire engine– and then, he saw her.

She lay in the grass, tree limbs draping her in flickers of moonlight, and she held her side.

"Are you hurt?" he asked when he reached her.

She looked up and Daniel saw fear in her eyes.

"It's bad, but there'll be ambulances here soon. Where are you hurt?"

"My side." She moved her hands. Her blouse was torn with a dark above her hip. When Daniel raised the material he had to look twice. Something had hit her, a rock, a piece of metal, possibly a jagged piece of broken lumber. Under the amber lights of the parking lot the wound looked horrible. It wasn't bleeding. It was a puncture injury, black and oozing. Daniel removed his dress shirt, then his undershirt. He folded his undershirt and placed it against her side.

She flinched at the pressure. "I've got to get you to a hospital." But for a few moments, Daniel remained knelt beside her. He gave no mind being bare shirt in the cool autumn air, and as she lay her head on his shoulder, he gently wrapped his other arm around her petite frame.

"Are you a student?"

She nodded.

The roadway quickly filled with the pulsating strobes of police cruisers. The snapping sound of opening gurneys and slamming vehicle doors had everyone in the parking lot in a state of chaos. Three were already confirmed dead. A dozen others were seriously injured.

The young woman's body convulsed ever so slightly and she succumbed to Daniel's gentle embrace.

"Did you come alone?" he asked.

"My roommate, but she's disappeared."

"Do you live in the dorm?"

She sat up more erectly and gazed closely at his face. "No, we have an apartment off campus."

"You're feeling better now?"

"Not really. I feel sick. Look at all of that," she said.

"Looks bad, but you'll be okay for now. I promise, I'll be back. I'll get you to the hospital. I'm going over to help."

"No please. Stay here."

Her words stopped him dead. It was a cross between a plea and a command. Daniel didn't move. Even with the tragedy all about them, Daniel was spellbound by her voice and appearance. He saw her profile in the moonlight, as unblemished as a porcelain doll. She had a small nose and a delicate chin and when he saw her wet eyes again, he wanted to hold her tight until her anxiety passed away. In the next few minutes, in spite of the anguish and suffering still unfolding around the demolished stage, all sirens and human cries dissipated from Daniel's ears, and all he could feel was her breathing.

He put his dress shirt back on as a frantic young woman ran up to them. "Where have you been? There are dead people over there. Why aren't you helping?"

"Not now, Laura. I've been hit."

"Hit by what? Where?"

Laura gave Daniel a disgusted glance, then continued her recriminations. "It's terrible over there, Margaret. I thought you were at the bottom of that wreck. What happened to you?"

"I got hit in the side by something. He's helping me."

Laura took a deep breath, and her mind changed gears. What she had witnessed was more than she could take. She knelt in the grass and began talking.

"It's terrible. It's terrible. The school will never live this down, I'm telling you. This is all this school will ever be known for." If Laura had any intention to return to the carnage to help, the notion evaporated from her thoughts. Instead, she closed her eyes and shook her head. "Not much that can be done now, I suppose. There's a lot of students over there completely dazed. I wish I hadn't looked."

"Why don't I get you to my car? It's just on the other side of this dorm." Daniel said. He helped the young woman from her position on the grass. "I'll get you to the emergency room."

"We're roommates. This is Laura."

But Laura wasn't listening. She relived the horror of the carnage she witnessed. "Damn, stupid jocks and their fraternities plotting to steal another school's mascot. How childish–how, how stupid can you get? I saw them take away Mary Driscoll in an ambulance, too. Oh, Margie, what are we going to do?"

"Get up," she said. "We need to go."

Daniel extended his hand to Laura, but she didn't take it. She got up from the grass on her own. The three of them walked to his car.

The hospital emergency room entrance was a

scene of complete bedlam. Daniel got a wheelchair from inside the door. Once inside, they spoke to a nurse, but she would have to wait. Her injury was non-life threatening. Laura paced the halls, then went back to the car to lie down. Daniel found room in the corner where he rolled her wheelchair, and he knelt beside her as they waited.

"Do you feel any better now?" Daniel asked.

"Yes, yes, I do. Thanks so much for staying with me. When I saw that fire engine hit the stage . . ." Her voice trailed off and she touched her side. "Then I felt the pain. I'm sorry I acted like a baby."

Daniel reached his hand under her chin and lifted her face to his gaze. "You're not a baby, and you didn't act like one."

"Well, I felt like one. I'm really glad you were there."

"And your name is Margaret?"

"Or Margie, if you like."

"That's such a beautiful name."

"Ahhh," she said. "I bet all girls' names are beautiful to you when you first meet them."

And with those words, Daniel became speechless and watched as a scared and trembling girl transformed into a gorgeous woman. Even in her discomfort, his presence braced her, and an ever so touching light adorned her face. Her eyes lit up, reflecting pools of warm caramel. Her lips opened with a pained, yet affectionate smile. She took his hand. "You're a knight in shining armor."

"You are feeling better then?" Daniel smiled. "Will I get to see you again after tonight? That is, if they don't cancel school."

"Maybe. I go to the student union every day."

They gazed into each other's eyes. He didn't move, took her other hand in his, and continued to gaze at her in the halo of light from the waiting room. He felt unable to move. He wanted to hold her tight, caress her once again. He wanted to place a long, warm kiss on her delicate lips. "I guess I should properly introduce myself. "My name is Daniel–Daniel King."

A thankful expression of warmth filled her eyes. "Yes–I know."

CHAPTER TWO

The carnage at Atherton University made the national news. The final count was five dead and thirty-three injured badly enough to need medical attention. Among the dead was the athletic director, a thirty-five-year-old father of three. He was thrown into the air and landed on his head on the asphalt parking lot. MacArthur State's bison head became a mass of shredded cow hide. Many wanted to cancel school for the remainder of the fall semester. The Atherton University president, at a midnight press conference, squelched any talk of cancellations. Trauma and despair would be strung out. No healing would occur unless everyone faced the tragedy with stiff resolve. Monday would be a day of mourning. Classes would resume on Tuesday.

When Daniel returned to the athletic dorm he

learned no one on the football team had been injured. Clint Stocker, an offensive lineman, carried around a broken stake he claimed had barely missed him as it flew past. Everyone on the team knew there would be no game tomorrow, though the official announcement didn't come until midnight. There were two more games on the 1990 schedule, one at home and the last one away. Daniel hoped those games would be played. Either way, he knew this season would be his last.

This night made him realize how precious life was. Football hardly pinged the radar of what was meaningful in life. He certainly wanted to play in two more games before he hung up his jersey, but when it came to what was important in life, he was more than sure he had met her tonight.

Five days later, Daniel caught sight of her in the student union. He watched her pick up her mail and proceed to the basement where tables for study and conversation were plentiful. Daniel followed and watched with a sense of awe and joy. She moved with such grace and poise. He felt a longing in his chest and he couldn't imagine another young woman being as beautiful.

She took a small table with two chairs and opened her mail.

"Is this chair taken?" he asked.

She looked up and her eyes brightened. "Oh, Daniel."

For a moment they gazed at one another. "I

wondered if you'd find me." A playful, impish glint brightened her eyes and lit her whole face.

"I've been looking for you every day."

"Well then, I'll give you an A for tenacity."

"It was hardly a chore," he said. "I'd call it a personal quest."

She smiled, an expression of acceptance layered with curiosity. "And now you've found me."

"Yes, Margie, I have. You're pleased, am I right?"

She paused as though thinking, but he knew she was glad he had.

"I do like you, Daniel."

"And I think you're adorable."

She laughed. "You certainly get to the point."

"How did you know my name the other night?"

Laura and I go to all the football games–Laura to see boys in the stands. I go to see the games. I didn't actually know your name but I knew you were on the team. There's a sharp picture of you in the program."

Daniel nodded. "I hadn't thought of that. You know, Margie, it's terrible what happened the other night, but I can't help but feel good about meeting you. The way it came about doesn't matter to me. I hardly know you but I can't get you out of my mind."

"My, my you are direct."

"Funny you should say that. My friends think I'm too easy going and don't speak up."

Margie looked at him closely. "A big boy like you?" She acted quite interested. "I don't mind you being direct."

"How about dinner then? I'll take you downtown to some nice place."

"You know we both have meal tickets to the cafeteria."

"Okay, I'll take you on a date to the cafeteria."

Again she laughed. "How can a big guy like you be so sweet?"

Daniel knew her words could be nothing more than friendly conversation, but the way she spoke let him know they were on the road to greater things.

"I'm being honest, Margie. I want to get to know all about you."

"Okay, Daniel. I have two classes this afternoon. In fact, my finance class starts in ten minutes so I must run." She grabbed up her books. "If you want to go downtown tonight, pick me up at my place around six." With that she stood and pressed her fingers to her lips. She didn't throw the kiss his way, but it all meant the same. He sat filled with a feeling, an emotion, he'd never experienced before as he watched her climb the stairs. He sat back and dwelt in a warm sensation in his chest as though he was becoming as light as air and was about to drift from the chair.

Daniel was at her door fifteen minutes before six. Margie opened it immediately, all ready to go. He saw she wore no makeup. Nothing he noticed, not even lipstick. And yet, she was beautiful. More beautiful than he could have ever imagined.

"I had a feeling you'd be early," she said.

"Is that all right?"

"Certainly, we have a date. I'm looking forward to it."

He drove a four-door Chevy, a car his father handled down. It wasn't built for intimacy, rather it seemed as wide as a 747 that could carry a little league baseball team. Yet, if Margie was assessing anything about him it wasn't his car or his clothes or where he would take her for dinner. He felt that she wanted to know as much about him as he did about her.

To that end, he knew better than to take her to the restaurant in an expensive hotel. His wallet couldn't stand it and she'd find such a display pretentious. He drove to a family restaurant on the outskirts of downtown Atherton.

When they were seated he asked, "what would you like to have?"

"Oh, anything is fine. Why don't you order for me?"

Instantly, he was perplexed, but then he smiled. "I don't know what you like. Is this a test?"

"No," she feigned a pout. "I'm sure I'd like whatever you choose."

"I like liver."

"So do I. That's perfect," she said as she unfolded a napkin and placed it in her lap.

"Ugh! I'm kidding. I can't stand to even smell the stuff."

She laughed in her childlike, innocent way. "I don't like it either," she admitted as she gazed at him with a look of growing interest.

"How about a ribeye or a chicken salad?"

"Either one sounds fine."

He ordered two chicken salads and they waited for their meals over sips of iced tea.

"I'm sorry I didn't ask in the student union, but how is your side?"

"I've got a black and blue bruise the size of a baseball, but it doesn't hurt unless I touch it."

"Maybe I should kiss it and make it better."

"I'm sure you'd like to."

"My kisses have magical powers." He gave her a sly smile, then got serious when she remained quiet with eyes down and squeezed the lemon slice into her tea. "Anyone you know get hurt?" he asked.

"One girl in my government class has a broken arm. I don't know her name but I've seen her in a cast. What about you?"

"My roommate from my first year here is in the hospital. His name's Greg, can't remember his last name. Anyway he got a punctured back and a collapsed lung, I think. I'll have to go see him. He was a nice guy."

"Oh, here's our food."

Daniel looked back across the table. He could tell Margie was a fun girl, but practical and down-to-earth. She would laugh at something truly funny, but would undoubtedly dismiss someone whose humor devolved into silliness. He watched her eat. She wasn't picky, but she had a way of preparing every mouthful. When he looked at her, her eyes were down. But when he looked up from his food, her eyes were on him.

"You have a beautiful head of hair," she said.

"Thanks. My dad still has most of his.

"Tell me about your family."

"Well, my dad is a sound engineer with Sony. My mom's a first-grade teacher. I have an older brother by two years, and another brother and sister, both in junior high."

"And you're a senior, right? That's what the football program said."

"Yes. Finishing up four years at good old Atherton U."

"What do you plan to do when you graduate?"

"My major is business. I'd like to get on with a fortune 500 company–be one of the thousands of mid-level anonymous faces that keep the wheels of business in motion. I figure it would be challenging enough work–decent pay."

"What about you, Margie? What do you want to do when you get out of here?"

"I'm still thinking about that. I'm only a sophomore."

"You've been around campus for a year and a half and I've never seen you? I must be blind. What have you been doing, taking all of your classes by correspondence course?"

"Oh no, Daniel. I've been around all this time. You've probably been too busy cracking heads at football practice. But you see me now. Am I right?"

The way she said it made him blink. Her captivating facial expression drew him like a magnet and he knew Margie was the whole package. He reached across the table and took her hand. "Margie, I'm so happy when I'm with you."

She put down her fork and dabbed the edge of

her mouth with a napkin. Her eyes were full of life and mischief. "Hold on a second, Casanova."

"What did I say?"

"Don't you think I probably have a boyfriend?"

"Do you?"

She paused and did that tilt with her head. "Not at the moment."

Daniel beamed. "See, problem solved."

They were back at the duplex by 8:30.

"I had a lovely evening," Margie said.

"So did I." And they softly shared their first kiss.

CHAPTER THREE

The Wildcats played their last two football games, but the home game was hardly attended. Margie was there and she cheered for the Wildcats as though there were 20,000 others with her in the stands. In the final away game, Daniel made five tackles and knocked down a pass. Still, the team lost each of their final two games.

From then until the Christmas break, Daniel and Margie were regularly seen together. He would pick her up in the morning, no matter how early, and take her to class. He would be with her in the evenings until he had to be back in the dorm. They called each other every day during the Christmas break. The three-week separation between semesters without Margie had Daniel an emotional wreck. Never in his life had three weeks lasted so long.

In January, Daniel began his final semester of classes to complete his degree. Margie was a sophomore and still completing required underclassmen courses. Neither of them gave serious discussion to the fact that Daniel would be leaving the school by summer.

The first Sunday they were back at school, Margie insisted Daniel pick her up for church. It was a reasonable request. Daniel wasn't a stranger to the church pew. His family regularly attended church and he knew all the Bible stories. Though his attendance in recent years had been a bit sporadic, he felt proud as he escorted Margie into the chapel. The church was an edifice of sandstone blocks. The thirty-foot-high gable entrance was inlaid with a round stained glass window, high on the wall, of a dawning sun illuminating a cross.

Daniel enjoyed singing traditional Gospel hymns. Margie's voice was light and beautiful as a Meadowlark singing at dawn. Daniel listened attentively to the sermon. The topic was about 'being apologetic.'

"Whenever you have a misunderstanding with a friend, co-worker, or relative, take responsibility whether you were right or wrong. A sincere apology has tremendous power." The minister continued, "For when you apologize, even when it's the last thing on earth you want to do, it relieves all stress and sets you free. The other person can't be grieved any longer and a relationship is healed. Sincere apologies are uplifting. No one can make you do it, but when you do, you are the stronger person. You will feel good, relieved, and understand you made the right decision."

The congregation prayed. As the prayer leader spoke from the pulpit, Daniel thought about his own private prayers. He prayed for students and faculty still recovering from the homecoming debacle. He prayed for the school and he prayed for Margie. Lastly, he prayed for himself.

After church services, Daniel and Margie went back to her duplex. No sooner had they entered, Margie went to the bedroom and took off her dress. Daniel watched and completely forgot what they had been talking about. She removed her jewelry and pantyhose, and stood for a moment in the middle of the bedroom in a bra and panties. She stepped to him, helped him remove his suit jacket and kissed him passionately.

Then, with a beckoning finger, Margie stepped back toward the bed. Daniel pulled off his tie and managed to kick off his shoes and loosen his belt before he fell into the bed still wearing his dress shirt, underwear, and socks. He kissed her and gazed into her eyes–eyes of total acceptance and complete surrender. She had decided to accept him. And though totally unexpected, Daniel was ready for her. His body yearned for her touch and they swam together in mutual ecstasy. For his motivation was affection and his caress was gentle.

At first, he frantically removed his shirt, but then

his frenzy slowed. There was time enough for a thousand kisses and all that followed was slow, loving, and passionate. Her skin was soft, yet firm. The faint scent of her perfume drifted around them, but the sweet smell of her body and her tender sighs mesmerized him. When they were spent, exhausted and sweaty, they lay beside one another and stared at the ceiling. Daniel hadn't realized prayers were answered so quickly.

Finally, Margie got up and covered herself with a robe. Daniel slipped from the bed, put on his shorts, and began searching the bed for coins that had spilled from his pants pockets. Margie watched and laughed.

"Are you looking for loose change?" Her laugh was an innocent sound of amusement with no condemnation.

Daniel instantly placed the coins he'd collected on the nightstand and ceased his search of the sheets. He glanced sheepishly in her direction and she smiled.

CHAPTER FOUR

Margie asked Daniel to go to San Angelo with her to attend the wedding of her best friend from high school. Margie was to be the maid of honor. The wedding was scheduled for Saturday, a month away, but they would need to go on a Wednesday to be there for activities preceding the important event. The whole idea sounded great to Daniel. He could skip a few classes and make arrangements to be off work from his janitor job at a nearby hospital.

Margie didn't have a car at school so they headed for San Angelo in Daniel's wide-body 1986 Chevy. Daniel listened to Margie's soft voice tell stories about her and the bride, Cynthia Bradshaw. The lilt in her voice rose with a hint of laughter as she told a story of them putting $5 worth of coins in the cafeteria jukebox and playing 'Heaven is a Place on Earth,' twenty times. It only cost twenty-five cents per spin, but no other song could play until their selection had played out. Everyone in the lunchroom liked the song for the first ten plays, then it became monotonous. Finally, someone pulled the plug on the machine. Margie and Cynthia had finished lunch, but sat where they were laughing under their breath all the while.

Daniel met Margie's mother, a friendly and loving woman. She fixed them delicious homemade meals when they weren't attending wedding functions. Margie's father had passed away several years earlier. Margie showed Daniel around her hometown of San Angelo.

The wedding was held at the Christian Church and the sanctuary was nearly full. Daniel sat halfway back, his eyes fixed on Margie. She was poised and absolutely beautiful. The women wore pink dresses and carried bouquets of pink and white flowers. Before the minister spoke, The bride's father stood to address those gathered. His speech about married life and commitment was heart-felt, well thought-out, full of words of wisdom for his daughter and new husband. Daniel listened intently. He would be standing beside a similar altar someday, and he knew it would be with Margie. He wasn't ready to get married, but the woman who would be standing opposite him was not in question. The way he felt about the future was the way Margie felt. If he were ever confident of anything in the world it was that someday Margie would be his wife.

When the reception line finally ended, and everyone took their seats for cake, toasts, and an open dance floor, Cynthia went down the line to give each of her attendants a special gift. Each received a pink opal brooch, half inch wide, set in silver petals. It was a beautiful item of jewelry for business or church attire. Rob, her new husband, gave all the groomsmen a white opal tie tack on a silver chain.

As cake was served and champagne flowed a number of people stood to make a toast. Margie was among that group. She had plenty of good things to say about Cynthia and was glad to do so.

"Hold this for me, will you?" she asked Daniel as she handed him the brooch in a jewelry case. "I don't have any pockets and I have to say a few words," she whispered in his ear. Daniel put the brooch in his jacket pocket.

Margie stood and looked around the room. "I've known Cynthia since we began junior high together. If it weren't for her, I'd have never made it through ninth grade algebra. If it weren't for Cynthia, I wouldn't have spent an entire night alone at Lake Nasworthy because she went off and left me." The assembly laughed. "But over the years, she's been my best friend, not only because we got along, but because she will do anything for a friend in need. I love you both and I wish you many years of happiness." Margie raised her glass and clinked it with Daniel's and the man sitting next to her.

When they headed back to Atherton, Daniel said, "That was a beautiful ceremony, Margie. I enjoyed meeting your mother. I'm glad you asked me to come."

Margie smiled and laid her head on his shoulder. "Yes, I'm so happy for Cynthia. It was a beautiful ceremony."

As the miles passed by, they sat in serene silence. Daniel thought of asking Margie about the recovery of her sorority sisters that were injured in the homecoming fiasco, but he didn't. That was a sad and touchy subject, hardly something to discuss after a wonderful four days. Daniel glanced at her. Margie stared out the windshield, her eyes on the road, her mind apparently somewhere else. Maybe Margie was thinking about her mother, all alone these days. Daniel admitted to himself he liked the woman, but what else could he ask about? He could ask her what she'd like to do this evening when they got back, but he would wait until they got closer to home.

Margie sat quietly and thought of her upbringing on a farm outside of San Angelo. When she was born, her two brothers and sister were all eight years or older. Her mother was the embodiment of the female spirit that won the west. She cooked three meals a day, washed the filthy clothes of three males, canned peaches, pears, and apples for the winter, read to the children when they were young, and got everyone up and to church every Sunday morning.

Her father treated her mother like a queen. Margie smiled when she saw her parents kiss. You can live anywhere and do anything for a living if you love and respect your mate. Margie knew her future life would be as happy and fulfilling as her dreams.

Occasionally she would look Daniel's way, but then, went back to her daydreaming.

Actually, all she was thinking about was Daniel. Once they got on the road, the man didn't utter a peep. He had witnessed two young people joining their lives in matrimony, and apparently it impressed him as much as a routine baseball game. She wished he'd bring up the subject. Even if they spoke in generalities and future intentions, Margie wished he'd think about being a husband. Taking a wife was not just another date. She wished he'd talk of things beyond college. She wanted him to talk like an adult and a husband.

For his part, Daniel wished Cynthia and Rob all the best, though he didn't really know them at all. His involvement in such functions for the foreseeable future would be limited to buying gifts and attending ceremonies. He felt sure Margie was of a similar frame of mind. Graduation was first on the list of priorities. Getting a job was second. After that, he and Margie would discuss matrimony. There was no hurry. Margie was already by his side. They were a couple. All the while, Margie gazed vacantly out the window as a herd of black Angus cows passed from view.

CHAPTER FIVE

In the spring of his senior year in 1991, Daniel lived the life of a twenty-two-year-old college student with no obligations, with an abundance of hours that spun five months into a lifetime. He was seldom in the dorm. His days on the gridiron were over. No more workouts, practices, or meetings. Most of the time he was with Margie. They attended several concerts at the Atherton City Auditorium and spent many hours riding bicycles along the residential streets around campus in the pleasant Texas' evenings.

Margie was always there. Or he was always with her, it seemed. Besides classwork and their part-time jobs, they had plenty of extra time. But they never discussed anything substantial. Adult issues didn't matter as long as Margie was around. Decisions on major topics could wait for another day. For Daniel, the spring of his senior year felt the way the rest of his life should be. He had to make a decision on the line of work he'd pursue, but other than that, important decisions could be made down the line.

Atherton had a hundred-acre lake north of the city. Homes dotted the eastern shore along with fishing piers and boat docks. But the western side of the lake was nothing but sandhills and prairie grass. The lake received a constant supply of water from a creek up north and the lake overflowed through narrow rivulets in the sand hills. Springtime warmed quickly in Texas, but the day was not hot. A soft breeze blew and the sky so high you could see forever without a cloud in sight.

Daniel and Margie traveled to the lake and drove across the numerous vehicle tracks in the sand. They were not there to swim or boat; just to be alone. They parked near a particularly wide eddy. In their swimsuits, they sat in the stream, the bubbling swirl of the water refreshing and relaxing. Margie lay across the stream, her body covered by water, and Daniel stretched out beside her.

The sun shone brightly. A slight breeze fluttered the prairie grass. The quiet afternoon was inspirational, and Margaret's touch instilled Daniel with such serenity he never wanted to leave that spot. After a time, he rolled on his side, gazed into her trusting eyes and kissed her.

"Have I told you how beautiful you are?"

"Yes. You've said that before."

"Can I say it again?"

She only nodded. Her expression was pensive, and if Daniel had been paying attention, he would have noticed the wanting in her eyes for further words of affection.

A roar of engines broke the silence as they huddled in the stream. It was a pack of four-wheelers attacking the dunes, and they passed them by without incident. They dried off and prepared to leave. Margie remained pensive, quiet, somewhat melancholy. Daniel didn't notice.

Back at her duplex, she turned on the TV and made sandwiches. Daniel got caught up in a movie and didn't budge from the couch. Margie went to the other room and did her schoolwork.

It was dark outside when the movie ended and Daniel went into the bedroom.

"One helluva movie," he said.

"I'm glad you liked it."

"Well, I better git. Busy day tomorrow."

"Daniel?"

"Yes."

"I had a wonderful time today."

"Me too, Margie." And he gave her a quick kiss on the forehead and left.

Laura showed up at the duplex twenty minutes later. She had evening classes, but could as easily have been at a friend's dorm room. She was at college to have fun. Meeting new people was her highest priority. Laura was a big girl with huge breasts for a nineteen-year-old. She had long brown hair, an engaging smile, and a mouth that spoke her mind.

"So where's super jock?" were the first words out of her mouth when she entered the bedroom. "He didn't want to help you study?"

Margie looked up from her work. "So Laura, what's on your mind?"

"Oh nothing. Just wondered where your pet was?"

"You must have had a dull night?"

"Yeah, could have been better. Got caught in Katie Thompson's room–you know Katie, right? A bunch of freshmen barge in her room and start talking about the silliest, junior high, bubble gum crap. I felt like telling them all to grow up. You're in college for crying out loud–act like it."

"I imagine you got in a few choice words."

"Not really, but I wanted to. So where's darling Daniel? It's not even ten o'clock."

Margie sat back in her chair. "He left fifteen minutes ago, if you must know.

"Oh yes, I must know. I'm your guardian angel, Margie, I know you think he's a dreamboat, but I'm here to tell you, he's just a jock."

"What's that supposed to mean?"

"Been hit in the head one too many times, has a one-track mind . . ."

"That's enough. You don't know anything about him."

"Huh? Wanna bet? He's the type of guy who wants to be out with the boys. I'm telling you– hunting birds in the fall, fishing in the spring, poker every Thursday night. Even if you asked, he'd never bring the boys over to play cards at your place. Oh no. Always at some bachelor pad, I'm telling you, so they can tell each other vulgar jokes. So many guys treat their woman like a trophy, but instead of raising you over their head, they escort you by the arm."

"You're so cynical, Laura. You'll never get married with that attitude."

"I know what I'm saying. I've seen it with my older brother and my dad. It's a shame how some men, without being mean or abusive, can still be so neglectful.

"Well, I've got a married older brother and he's a perfect gentleman."

"I'm trying to clue you in, Margie. Daniel may not be at the bottom of the barrel, but he's not at the top either. Find yourself a guy in pre-med or accounting, or architecture. Nothing says you can't find someone to love that makes a lot of dough."

"Okay Laura. Now you can go mind your own business. I wish you'd have read the riot act to those freshmen girls to get all the venom out of your system."

"I'm not vindictive, Margie. Call it advice worth considering. How long have you been seeing him? Four months? Five months? I know it was before Christmas, oh yeah, that night before homecoming. In all this time, has he ever surprised you? Bought you something unexpected? Taken you someplace new or out of the ordinary? Huh? Has he?"

Margie dropped her gaze and slowly closed a book. "Daniel is as sweet as they come and I know he cares for me."

Chapter Six

Daniel and Margie took a weekend trip to San Antonio. They took a boat ride on the canal along the city's riverwalk. Daniel took pictures of Margie at every turn in the river, every outdoor restaurant, even in the lobby of their hotel. Their stop at the Alamo was inspiring for both of them. In the courtyard as she sat on a knee-high stone wall, Daniel took the picture that would become his absolute favorite. Foliage surrounded her as sunlight lit her face. Her poise, the beauty of her dainty features caressed by hair as dark as black silk shown like a single star in the heavens. They stopped in New Braunfels on their way back to Atherton and went tubing down the Guadalupe River. They floated with dozens of others in tractor tire inner tubes down the gentle rapids. They were physically spent when they reached the duplex.

Daniel awoke in the middle of the night and

found Margie lying over his right arm. Her head rested on his shoulder. Her chin brushed his chest as her face nestled in the curve of his neck. He dared not move lest he wake her.

In the quiet darkness of the room he could hear her breathing, and it was as though he could hear the beating of her heart. Daniel lay quietly and inhaled her smell. Margie wore a T-shirt top and her panties. Daniel was in a pair of briefs. They had arrived home so exhausted, they took showers, and each one fell into bed–half asleep before they hit the mattress. Daniel smiled when he thought about their whirlwind weekend, and he kissed her head, and closed his eyes.

The next day, Daniel mentioned an idea he'd been mulling over for some time.

"Margie, I've decided what I want to do."

Margie had been moving about the kitchen, but stopped and leaned attentively across the counter.

"I had a really interesting conversation with a recruiter."

Margie stepped from behind the counter. "Good," she said. "Tell me all about it."

"The Atherton Police Department is hiring. The tenth largest city in the state. Their pay package is great."

Margie took a step back. Her face turned white. "You want to be a cop?"

"Community service, Margie. Giving back. I'll have my diploma. I've got the physical traits they're looking for. They'll accept me, for sure."

"I don't care how strong you are, Daniel, you

can't take a bullet."

"Police work is something new every day," he said.

"Something new a hundred times over, Daniel. Giving a ticket to someone speeding in a school zone one day, arresting a shoplifter another. You call that exciting?" Margie was now in his face, but he could see, she was not angry–she was afraid.

"Margie, I can't see myself in an office or stuck in a store."

"You haven't signed any papers, have you–put in an application?"

"No. None of that. It's all preliminary. I wanted you to know. I thought you'd be excited."

"Excited isn't the word, Daniel. More like a heart attack. You think being out in public is exciting? What about a call to a domestic disturbance–those words scare the hell out of me. You could get injured by either party in one of those brawls."

Daniel was out of rebuttals. It was a bit scary to see Margie worked up so much. Her eyes were penetrating, arms folded, in a no-nonsense stance. Daniel hadn't seen this side of Margie and he was both surprised and amused. There's some fight in that girl to go along with a bright mind and a damn cute smile. "If you don't want me to follow-up on that job opportunity; I won't."

"You have other offers, right?" she asked.

"Yeah. They're worth looking at again, I suppose."

"Let me go through them with you, Daniel. A second opinion, okay?"

Daniel didn't answer. Margie came over and sat

beside him and took his hand.

"Honey, look at me– Don't you think your job prospects are something we should talk about together?"

"Sure, babe."

"And most of them will require relocation. We'd want to talk about that too."

"I'm sorry I upset you." A long pause hung between them.

"You're doing fine, Daniel King," and she put her arms around his neck and kissed him on the cheek.

A week later, Clint Stocker pulled Daniel aside after a business law class. "Who do you think I met last night?"

"The governor of Texas."

"You know a girl named Laura Becker?"

"Yes, what about her?"

"Met her over at Martin's house. His girlfriend was there, some new chick I hadn't met before, and me and Laura."

"Where was Sara?"

"Back in the dorm, I suppose. But nothing happened. I'll never cheat on Sara. We're getting married as soon as I graduate. Sara's my girl and I tell her that every day."

"So, I guess my name came up?"

"Oh yes, Laura has definitely been keeping tabs on you."

Daniel shrugged. "Yeah, I can imagine. Why

was I a topic of conversation?"

"We all had a few beers and she was doing the talking, so we let her talk. The way she was carrying on you're just a bundle of hormones and an empty skull."

"I really don't want to hear about it."

"Yeah, you do. Listen bro, Laura's full of negativity about your girlfriend too."

"What did she say about Margie?"

"Laura wasn't all that complimentary of your girlfriend either. She thinks Margie's making a big mistake with you. I don't know. Maybe Laura's jealous. Maybe she's just a meddler. But a word to the wise, bro. You take a woman for granted at your own peril."

Clint continued. "I'm telling you, God put women on this earth for two reasons–for men to love and be frustrated by. Come on, let's get out of here." The hallway was full of students chattering as they moved down the corridor. "You've got some time, right? Let's go over to McDonald's."

The two young men sat with their sodas in a corner booth. Daniel was the first to speak.

"I compliment Margie all the time."

Clint stretched his arms across the restaurant booth, then folded his hands over the table and leaned in. "It's complicated, man. Women aren't just pretty and soft and sexy. They're wired differently, bro. A successful relationship with a woman is a full-time job."

"And you know all of this because you have Sara under your spell?" Daniel smiled.

"Listen, man. Women's brains are always turning, wondering, planning, conniving. They only take a rest when they're sleeping and I'd swear their dreams keep the process going. You can't be superficial with your compliments of a woman. You have to be specific. You have to be sincere. And you have to be emotional."

Clint was on a roll. Daniel was his captive audience while he spouted his limited knowledge of the fairer sex. "Take Sara, you bring her up. I love her to the moon and back, and I tell her. You know, a woman will follow a man she loves to the top of a mountain and live in a log cabin or move to a farm and be around nothing more than plowed ground, cattle pens and chicken coops, if, and only if, she feels that man loves her. And one way you convey that is with time and attention." Clint leaned across the table to where Daniel had to look him in the eye.

"Daniel, do you love Margie?"

"Damn, of course I do. I think she's great. She's my girl and she knows I'll always be there for her." Daniel shrugged his shoulders but sat up straight. "It's really none of your business."

Clint fell back in the booth and scratched his head. "But do you tell her?"

For a minute the two young men sat in silence. Then, Clint pulled himself back up to the table.

"I don't know where to begin," Clint said. "Women soak up compliments like a sponge. Without them, they get bitter and feel neglected. What do you think college is–Neverland? Do you think there's a better place to find an intelligent, good-looking girl than here? If you can't express heartfelt emotion, maybe you don't care about her as much as you say and you need to come clean and move on."

"It's not like that. I think the world of Margie. I want to be with her, and I will be," Daniel said. "On your terms. Now I'm getting what Laura was talking about. You like the relationship as long as it pleases you. I thought you were a straight up dude, but stringing out some girl who cares about you isn't being straight up."

"Come on, Clint. What's your major, marriage counseling? I haven't even graduated yet. You're trying to pin me down when I don't even have a job lined up. What am I supposed to say?"

"Yeah, but when you love someone, you tell them. If you don't, I guess you don't. No wonder Laura says Margie's confused and unhappy."

"Okay, I'll tell her I love her," Daniel said.

"Man, you don't really sound like it." Clint slurped at the ice in his cup then evidently had an epiphany. His eyes lit, he leaned forward in his seat, and pounded his fist into his other hand. "I've got it. This is it. Go get a ring. Get on your knees, propose, and play it up. An engagement can last as long as you want, but at least you'll have a horse collar on her until you make up your juvenile mind."

"That's a crude way of putting it, not to mention the dumbest thing I've ever heard. I'm not about to play with Margie's emotions that way."

"I'm just trying to break through to you, bro. Being proposed to is what most women dream about. If she says 'yes', you have a winner. If she says 'no', better to know now than later."

"Wow. I don't know why I'm listening to this. I

certainly don't want Margie to say no. When I propose, it will be at the right place, the right time, the right setting.

Besides, I think Laura runs her big mouth to get attention. Margie and I are a couple. There's nothing I won't do for her, and she knows it. Thanks for the pep talk, Clint, but you're missing a lot. I can handle it. Margie is a sweetheart. I can handle it."

CHAPTER SEVEN

Instead of biking, some evenings Daniel and Margie would take walks along a wide median with benches placed every twenty yards or so along a row of bushes. They walked quietly hand in hand. They took a bench and spent a moment gazing at the stars. Margie turned to Daniel and took his hand.

"Sweetheart, where do you see yourself in five years?"

Daniel sat up straight. "That's a good question, babe." He paused. The question was not one he'd contemplated. "To tell you the truth, I don't really know. I should, I know, but I've just been thinking about a job." He shook his head. "Is that so bad?"

"Don't you have some sort of goal?"

"To have a nice house, I suppose, and a loving family. To be a good husband and father."

Margie squeezed his hand. "That's sweet, Daniel, and I know you mean it, but we're at a point in our lives where we have to plan for the future."

"Work and save, right?"

"That's part of it, but . . ."

Daniel pulled her to himself. "Margie, I will do everything for you. We'll build the future together."

Margie reclined on the bench and put her head in his lap and played with a dandelion between her fingers. "Atherton is a nice town, but I want to live in the big city," she spoke to Daniel as she gazed at the stars.

"Dallas is a big city," he said.

"Or Denver," she smiled up at him. "Wouldn't you like to live near the mountains?"

He brushed her hair with his hand. "Wherever you like, Margie. As long as I'm with you."

Her voice waxed nostalgic as if she recalled a dream. "My sweet, Daniel. You're always so agreeable. Don't you ever get upset?"

"I suppose so, but not often. I see no reason to get into an argument over something minor, and with bigger issues, I try to give the other person the benefit of the doubt."

Margie gazed up at him and smiled. "That's what you are–a big, soft teddy bear."

"Of course, if you're naughty, I can always give you a spanking." He began to turn her over in his lap.

"Daniel, no." Margie jumped to her feet.

"I think you need a spanking," he said. Then he paused. "Either that, or a kiss. What's it going to be young lady?

Margie sat back on the bench, leaned into Daniel, and gave him a warm, passionate kiss. They gazed into each other's eyes. "My sweet, Daniel," she said,

"Margie, you're the best," Daniel replied.

<hr>

The graduation ceremony was held on the Saturday afternoon immediately following the last day of classes. Daniel was excited and relieved to be wearing his royal blue cap and gown. His mother and father came in from Dallas along with his two younger siblings. The five of them ate lunch together but an evening meal was set aside for Daniel and Margie and his mother and father.

The keynote speaker was a man who owned a chain of restaurants and his talk was all about hustle and hard work, 'never quit, ' and 'failure gets you one step closer to your goal.' When Daniel walked across the stage and received his diploma he was filled with a satisfying sense of accomplishment. His years of study and hard work had paid off. Margie attended and watched with pride as Daniel received his embossed and signed sheepskin.

Margie met the King family in the parking lot and introductions were made. Everyone would have a few hours to rest up. Daniel and Margie would pick up his parents at their motel at six.

Daniel's mother was an outgoing woman with abundant questions. But none of her questions came across as a cross examination, but rather, as a pleasant conversation. The women were good friends before their meals arrived.

His father was more reserved. When the food arrived, his attention was focused on how best to cut his steak. He had lived with Daniel's mother for twenty six years. He knew when she got into one of her pleasant, chatty phases, it was best for him to just sit back and relax. The women did all the talking. It was apparent that his mother fully approved of Margie. Daniel's father didn't make such assessments. If the young lady made Daniel happy and was in his future as his bride to be, that was good enough for him.

All the while, Margie smiled and interacted with Mrs. King. She cut her food into pieces small enough for a bird to eat, her movements as delicate as a Hummingbird. In a different era, Daniel could see Margie wearing a pearl necklace and white gloves to the dinner table. Everytime she glanced his way, Daniel felt the euphoric warmth of her smile.

The spring semester had ended and the halls of the university assumed a summertime pace. Daniel neither accepted any of the jobs he'd interviewed for through the university nor left Atherton. He got a job at a funeral home. A friend of his worked there but went back home for the summer break. One of the homes in town hired college boys to ride shotgun on death runs and transport the sick and elderly to and from the hospital. The young men were less expensive than keeping a full time adult on staff. The boys lived in a cottage behind the funeral home and took turns being on night call.

Talk about something new every day. The bodies came like clockwork, six or seven a week. A child killed in a car wreck, a suicide, a murder victim with defensive cuts on his palms, old people, one after another, all races, both sexes, every age across generations.

Seeing a dead person he didn't know didn't bother him. The wrench in his emotions came when he had seen the person alive and then saw them dead. Picking up an older person at their home and taking them to the hospital began to make him sad every time. He rode with them in the back of the funeral home's ambulance and invariably they would speak to one another about something. Daniel soon learned there was a good chance he'd be picking them up a week or two later for a one-way trip to the prep room.

He also had to attend funeral services. He'd escort the family to the front of the chapel and lend a hand to anyone who needed assistance being seated. Then he waited at the back. He came to dread the services more than the death runs. No matter who had died, a teenager or some octogenarian, there was always someone in the family who wailed uncontrollably. "Come back to me, Marty." "My baby, my little baby, look at my Julie." When he heard the cries of absolute, unvarnished heartache Daniel was equally torn. He stood in the recess of the front door and wiped his eyes.

The absolute worst involved a man in his fifties who had died on the operating table while having a brain tumor removed. The home bought a wig to cover the man's sutured head. His head was mush to the touch as none of his removed skull had been replaced.

The service began as they always did, soft hynms playing through the sound system, shuffling feet, whispering voices here and there. When the family began to move past the casket, one woman, Daniel assumed was the man's wife, began a wail that only crescendoed when she got close enough to gaze upon the dead man's face.

"Phillip, don't leave me. Come back to me. Oh Phillip, my darling, my darling, don't leave me." Daniel knew the Fowlers, the funeral director and his son, would have their hands full with her the rest of the afternoon. It's no fun to listen to someone cry from the depths of their heartbroken soul. The woman was inconsolable. She hugged the coffin with both hands. His death must have been totally unexpected. Possibly, if he'd dropped unconscious in front of her in the middle of a conversation never to speak another word. But he had undergone an operation. There are always risks with medical procedures especially when it concerns the brain. Doctors sometimes make mistakes. Sometimes the human body can't be fixed. The woman's wails gave no hint she had the slightest thought her man was about to leave this world. Daniel stood in the back of the chapel as the sadness of the moment gripped him along with everyone else and he had to hold his handkerchief over the bridge of his nose to catch all the tears.

The woman would not ride in the family limousine. She insisted she ride with the coffin in the hearse. Randy, Daniel's roommate in the cottage, was assigned to ride with her. Daniel wouldn't wish that job on anyone. Randy was the sensitive sort. He had zero chance of consoling the woman during the ride. Before the hearse was halfway to the cemetery, Randy would be in mourning along with the woman and bawling like a baby.

While there was a serious and sad side to the funeral home, it also provided the perfect set-up for devious pranks. When Daniel got back to the cottage on his nights off, he checked the prep room to see if any new 'visitors' had arrived. The Fowlers were gone at night. In the viewing rooms, only the dead slept within the funeral home's walls. If someone were with him, Daniel would take them gently into the building as if he had to get something and steer them toward the prep room.

But no one accompanied Daniel with any notion that the place was anything less than a haunted house. It was, after all, a funeral home, and with Daniel's animated invitation, all who entered felt the hair rise on the back of their necks. The smell of formaldehyde hit when someone stepped through the back door. The place was eerie and dimly lit. His friends wanted the rush of artificial fear. When he brought Margie by at 11 p.m. after a movie, Margie agreed to go inside. Daniel could feel her excitement. He led her down a hallway where two candle shaped lights lit the far end of the corridor. He opened a door and coaxed Margie to move closer.

"Now Daniel, don't have me touching a dead body.

"Never, babe." Daniel held her close.

He flipped on the light. The room was filled with coffins, shiny red and gold metal from head to toe, polished mahogany, giant brass handles.

Margie sucked in her breath. "So beautiful and so eerie, Daniel. This gives me the creeps."

"Do you want to see how it feels to lay in one?"

Margie shuddered. "Don't do that." Her tone let him know she wasn't mad. It was one of those, 'I want to be scared but don't give me a heart attack.'

Daniel chuckled. "Let me show you something else."

"I don't know, Daniel. You're being mean."

"No, I'm not." He kissed her on the cheek. "It's all in fun."

He led her down another hall that took them to the prep room by another door. The funeral home didn't cover the bodies when they were on the slab, figured the modesty of the person in question wouldn't be offended.

The whole purpose of Daniel's guided tour of the funeral home was to instill a frightful chill in his guest. Daniel had been gone from the funeral home all day and had the night off. In that length of time, it was highly likely a deceased had come in. It could be anyone, in any condition. Often, Daniel was as surprised as the person he had with him. The door bottom creaked across the floor and added to a rising tension. Daniel flipped on the light. Margie stood wide-eyed, staring in disbelief. Daniel was caught mid-breath. It was the saddest sight he had ever seen. Daniel thought he'd seen it all from a six-year-old girl who died in a car wreck to a middle aged man who'd hung himself.

But the corpse in front of him almost brought him to tears. It was a young woman, no more than twenty. Her long reddish-blonde hair hung over the top of the porcelain slab. She reminded him of Margie. Though the eyes of the dead girl were closed and her skin now a waxy white, she was beautiful. The deceased was naked from head to toe. There wasn't a mark on her. Daniel quickly covered her with a sheet.

"I'm sorry, Sweetie. I didn't mean for you to see something like that."

"She's so pretty, so perfect," Margie said, almost to tears.

"And so young," Daniel shook his head and led Margie to the back door.

Neither of them mentioned the girl again. The next day, Daniel found out she'd overdosed.

CHAPTER EIGHT

Laura had left town for the summer. Margie remained at the duplex and took summer courses. Daniel would have asked to move in except that to work at the funeral home he had to live in the cottage. For Daniel, the spring had been magical. Margie was constantly beside him. They had no interests outside of what the other wanted to do. There was no doubt in his mind, Margie felt the same as he did about their future together. Daniel's assumptions filled in all the gaps for him. Margie was his girl. He knew it. All of his kisses, hugs, and smiles were for her. Daniel could express his feelings, he simply failed to do so. The words he spoke were void of whispered promises of eternal commitment. Margie wanted to hear him tell her she was the only one. She wanted to hear the magic word.

On an evening in July, when the scorching heat

of the day had subsided, Daniel took Margie to a downtown bar with a dance floor no bigger than a small bedroom. There were a dozen or so people in the place, but it felt dead. He held her close as they danced to a slow number. They had one drink apiece, then left the bar.

Back at the duplex they made passionate love. Daniel showered Margie with kisses during their lovemaking, especially on her neck. When their throws of ecstasy had subsided, Daniel rolled off of her faster than a drunk falling off a curb. He kissed her once again on the forehead. "You're the best, babe. You're the best."

Margie reached for him as he rolled off the bed.

He pulled on his pants. "I better go. Busy day tomorrow."

Margie pulled the comforter over her naked body, physically fulfilled for the moment, but emotionally sad and pushed her face into her pillow as she heard the front door close.

An old friend came to town and Margie went to dinner with him. He was a high school classmate who had just been discharged from the military. Robert Rucker took Margie to an upscale steakhouse. They ordered cocktails and sat in ambient candlelight.

Robert looked so sharp and poised with his short haircut and steady gaze. Margie was more than surprised when he showed up at the duplex the previous morning. Today, he had a beautiful bouquet of flowers sent to her at the duplex. It was nice to see him again, her high school sweetheart.

"I thought of you every day I was in the service, Margie. It's so good to be back in Texas."

"Did you see all of the world you wanted to see?" Margie asked with a smile.

"If the world is Oakland, California, then I saw plenty of it. We did spend six months in Hawaii." Robert reached across the table and took her hand. "Not only are you as beautiful as ever, but you must also know–my love for you has never faded."

Margie listened. The confession was so genuine, she couldn't make light of it. What could she say? Margie was starstruck and overwhelmed. Robert was a man. Daniel still treated life as an endless pass to Disneyland.

"I'll love you until the earth falls into the sun." And then, Robert slipped from his chair, and knelt on the floor beside their dinner table. He took from his pocket a jewelry box and opened it. "Margaret Winters, will you marry me?'

All eyes from nearby tables focused on Robert's performance, and the ensuing pause. Margie gasped and put her hand to her mouth, her eyes mesmerized by the box. The entire room went silent. The air in the room held its breath.

Margie's eyes welled up and she grabbed her hands together. She looked into Robert's hopeful expression. Margie was overcome with excitement and the words gushed from her lips. "Yes Robert, yes. I will marry you."

Two days later, Margie showed up at the cottage shortly after one. Daniel had a towel wrapped around him, standing at the mirror shaving.

"Margie, you should have called. I have to work a funeral in an hour."

She stood in the doorway, red eyed and withdrawn. "An old boyfriend of mine is back in town."

Daniel kept shaving as though he hadn't heard a word.

"He wants me to be with him," she said.

Daniel stopped, glanced her way, and rubbed the last of the shaving cream from his face.

"From here?"

"No, high school."

"If he's so fond of you, where's he been?"

"The Marines."

"Are you trying to make me jealous?" Daniel smiled, and stepped behind the door to put on his shorts.

"I'm going with him." Margie sobbed audibly now and she turned away.

"Come, come now, Margie. Whoever this guy is, he's old news. When did he get out?"

"Last month."

"Has he been writing to you all this time?"

"Some, in the beginning. He didn't have my address when I moved to Atherton."

"See," Daniel stepped to her and put his arms on her shoulders. "He's been subject to all that military right-face, forward march bullshit, he's ready to jump at the first woman who looks his way."

"He says he loves me, Daniel."

"Loves you. Ha! I love you. Does he know about me?"

"Yes."

"Well then, tell the SOB to take a hike."

"I'm going to go with him."

"Damn. You would throw this at me when I have to work. We need to talk this out."

"I'm going, Daniel. I have to go. I wanted to tell you in person."

"You'll be sorry, Margie. You'll be sorry."

Margie walked from the cottage constantly wiping her eyes. He could hear her muffled cries.

Daniel pulled on his dress pants and went back to the mirror and studied the closeness of his shave. "She'll be back. She'll be back."

You can love someone so much . . .

but you can never love them as much

as you can miss them.

<small>John Green</small>

CHAPTER NINE

The next day Daniel called. Margie didn't answer. He tried later. Still no answer. The following day, he called again. A message said the number was no longer in service. He had to be on call that night at the funeral home, but on the third day, Daniel went to the duplex. No one answered his knocks on the door.

He peered below the living room blinds and the sight drove a hollow chill into his bones. The apartment was empty. He went around to the bedroom window. The blinds were up. The mattress was still there but the bedding was gone. He could see into the closet. Her clothes were gone, as well.

He turned his back against the house, and slid to the ground. Seated in the blazing sun with his head in his hands, Daniel couldn't believe the turn of events. Hadn't he made love to her only days earlier? Hadn't he declared his affection? She might be upping the ante on the relationship. Maybe now Margie was playing hard-to-get. But the empty duplex told a story far different than the one he tried to imagine. An awareness gripped him and yanked him to earth as though, for the past six months, he'd been living in the clouds. Margie had left him, and the emotional trauma made him physically sick. His mind was frazzled. Where could she be? He would track down this ex-Marine and show him what a 'good man' could really do. But moments later, the weakness that had hit him earlier returned and he felt afraid. A jumble of thoughts attacked his brain and he made some quick decisions without a second thought. His life had hit a wall. His emotions were in tatters. Something terrible had happened and he intended to find out why. Daniel went back to the funeral home and immediately quit the job. He packed his stuff and moved back to Dallas. The day after he found an apartment, he submitted his application to the Dallas Police Academy.

His parents agreed to assist him with living expenses during his 28-week training. The classroom education was rigorous, the physical training demanding, and the firearms instruction comprehensive. All the hours of training helped him forget Margie.

Late in September, Daniel traveled south to watch the Wildcats play Sam Houston State. He got into the visitor's locker room, greeted old teammates, and did his part to fire them up for the game.

At halftime the Wildcats were leading by seven.

He saw Laura in the stands talking with a group of people. He recognized none of them. He was afraid to talk to her, but equally compelled. She possibly knew, had to know something about Margie. At this point, he didn't care if Margie had moved out of the country. He didn't care where she was or what she was doing–but he had to know.

He watched Laura leave her seat and walk to the concession area. He stood back and watched her order a soda and a giant pretzel. As she left the concession counter he walked up to her.

"Hello, Laura." He stood to her side, not blocking her path. Apprehension gripped him and he figured she'd tell him to drop dead. But when their eyes met, she gazed at him with an expression he couldn't interpret as anything but pity.

"Hello, Daniel."

"Long way to come to see a football game."

"Some friends invited me.

"When I saw you, I thought I could at least say hello."

"How are you doing, Daniel?" Her question was void of any true interest, but at least, she didn't excuse herself.

"I'm in Dallas now."

She nodded politely,

"Have you seen Margie?"

Again she nodded.

"Is she going to finish school?"

Her gaze was filled with sympathy as though those defeated in battles of the heart, at the very least, didn't deserve to be crushed further. "She's married now, Daniel."

She said it as gently as one can deliver such news, but the words hit him with a slap upside the head.

"Wow, pretty quick. Did you go to the wedding?"

"Yes, I did. Listen Daniel." She moved to the back of the concession area and took a sip of her drink. "I know there's no way you could have known I'd be here at this game. I didn't know myself until this morning. So, I understand why you came up to me. But–"

For a woman who could speak so harshly and directly, her hesitancy was disconcerting. He almost appreciated her behavior. She was trying to let him down easy.

"You have to forget, Margie. She's a married woman now."

"Are they going to live in San Angelo?"

Laura closed her eyes and slowly shook her head. "I think they've already moved and I don't know where."

"What's her last name?"

"Daniel, you're not listening. I'm not going to tell you that. If seeing me has brought back painful memories, I'm sorry. But there's nothing more for you to know. She's happy. She's moved on, and you have to, too."

Daniel sighed heavily and searched his brain desperately for something else to ask. A loud horn went off signaling the beginning of the second half.

"Time to go back to my seat. Look to the future, Daniel, and take care of yourself. I have to go."

He watched in silence as Laura turned and walked away.

Daniel completely forgot about the football game and walked to his car in a daze. Margie had said she was leaving with someone else. Her goodbye to Daniel was a statement of finality. But to learn she had gotten married less than two months later had him in shock, bewilderment beyond comprehension. His mind churned with so many rambling ideas he couldn't grasp a single thought. Nausea overtook him and he threw up in the parking lot. Why? How did this happen?

He thought he could deal with life's curveballs. But how does one cope when blindsided? He felt a simmering rage for any man who would steal another's girl. He had no inkling her leaving was about to happen. Why was Margie so cruel to dump him that way? He had to be in Dallas for Monday morning's academy roll call. His mind was not on driving during his trip back home, and he almost drove off the road several times. He couldn't make sense of her leaving, but he knew he'd never stop loving her.

CHAPTER TEN

For Margie, the encounter with Daniel at the cottage wrenched her body with shakes and sobs. She hadn't wanted to confront him that way. She wasn't happy she had. Nothing she had ever done in her life approached the anguish she felt as she told Daniel she was leaving. Even worse, she knew Daniel would be more confused than heartbroken because he wouldn't let himself believe it was true. That thought made her sadder.

She had made a decision borne of grandiose promises and whispered sweet nothings. Robert Rucker was a smooth operator. Military service had piqued his confidence. For one critical moment, he had gotten Margie to forget Daniel completely. Besides, she knew Robert, she cared for him. He would be a loving and attentive husband,

When Robert returned to civilian life, he intended to get what he wanted. The first thing he wanted was his high school steady, Margie. Upon being discharged he found out where she lived and drove directly to Atherton. At six o'clock one morning, he knocked on her door with hot coffee and breakfast sandwiches. He stayed until nine when she had to go to class. He was around her constantly when she wasn't in class, and took her to dinner the next evening.

Robert parked on the street. When Margie returned from her encounter with Daniel, Robert didn't ask a word about the conversation. But Margie confirmed what he wanted to know.

"I told him," she said.

Robert reached across the car seat and squeezed her hand. "I love you, Margie. No one could ever love you more. We're going to have a wonderful life together."

That night they cleaned out her belongings from the duplex. The next day they drove back to San Angelo.

Robert was intelligent and in shape. But he had only a high school education and his military training in the art of killing people with all manner of weapons had limited utility in the civilian world. He was a slender young man, nearly six feet tall. He had the body frame of a man who

would always be slender. His deep brown eyes matched his hair. He had broad shoulders but with little muscular definition. He was fit, but lean. His facial features were pleasant. There wasn't an ounce of fat on him.

Robert got a job with the Texas Department of

Transportation building roads. He was assigned to a road widening project of highway 290 west of Austin that connected the state capital to I-10. For two weeks Margie and Robert prepared for the move to South Central Texas.

Margie's mother lived in a small apartment for seniors. Margie's oldest brother now lived on and ran the family farm. The day after they arrived back in San Angelo, over morning coffee, Mrs. Winters probed Margie's thinking pertaining to her change of plans.

"Margaret, you know you can stay here during the summer, but I can't believe you're dropping out of school."

"I plan to go back, mother. I need a change in my life right now."

"Change of –what does that even mean, Margaret? If you don't complete your degree work now, the chances are, you never will."

"Mom, I'll be fine. Do you remember Robert Rucker? He's out of the military now,"

The older woman had to think for a moment. "Yes, I remember Robert."

"He proposed to me," Margie gushed.

Margie's face beamed as Mrs. Winters almost fell from her chair. Margie brought her left hand out from behind her back and showed her mother a small, yet glittering, diamond ring.

"Oh Margie, I don't know what to say."

Margie beamed. "Say congratulations, mom. Your baby girl is going to get married."

Mrs. Winters stared in disbelief as though she were talking to someone she didn't know. "But

Margie, you're barely twenty years old. Marriage is for a lifetime. Are you sure the time is right?"

Margie touched her mother's shoulder, then hugged her. "I'm sure, mother. I'm sure."

"What happened to that young man you brought to Cynthia's wedding? I thought you two got along nicely."

"Things change, mother. That's all I want to say about it. I'm going to marry Robert." Margie tilted her head in the cute manner of hers. "Margaret Rucker. Don't you think that sounds nice?"

Her mother ignored the question. "So you're not rushing to the altar just because Cynthia did?"

"Mother! I thought you'd be happy for me. No more questions–please. Robert and I have to leave for Fredericksburg in less than a week. I need you to make wedding arrangements here in town, for the early part of September. I can send out invitations from down there. We're going to have to arrange a wedding around his work schedule."

Mrs. Winters teared up. "Oh Margie. I am happy for you, married so soon, but I guess that means more grandchildren while I'm still healthy enough to enjoy them "

Margie knelt beside her mother and put her head in her lap. "Thank you, mama."

Around eighty people were in attendance at the wedding ceremony. Margie looked and acted as a precious princess in every sense of the word. She was gracious. She was attentive to everyone in the room. The tiny tilt of her head and the bright blue eyes gave witness to the emotion of her heart. On that day, Margie was in love.

But it wasn't long before she was bored stiff with her new accommodations in Fredericksburg, Texas. She had left her studies, her friends, and her childhood home. She heard more Spanish spoken around the apartment complex than anything else, and she wondered what she could do that was the least bit interesting with no degree, in a town where she knew absolutely no one.

By the end of the year, their nest egg saw significant gains. Robert took home $18.50 an hour after deductions, good money since they had next to no expenses besides food and rent. Margie began to keep a personal notebook. She smiled to herself, what could she possibly write about in this strange town. She began to write about Daniel.

What was Daniel doing today? He had graduated. She wondered if he stayed in Atherton. At first, it was fun to reminisce. She had been quite fond of that oversized boy with the thick hair and an engaging smile. She wondered, in exactly six months, where was he now?

What she saw of Robert at the end of each day was a sweaty, exhausted, and hungry man. Several times he fell asleep on the bed before he'd fully dried off or had put on any of his clothes. In the morning it was a quick kiss as she handed him a breakfast sandwich. He had to be on the job before the sun came up. They had little time for sex.

She cared for Robert but soon found they had different interests, different ideas. Margie enjoyed football. She understood the game from watching her brothers play—-and Daniel. If Robert was interested in any sports, it was college basketball and that was it. Margie quickly gave up on having him attend church with her. Sunday was a rest day, Sunday he could sleep. That's exactly what he did.

Out of the blue, Margie wrote in her journal about the Billy Joel concert Daniel had taken her to. The next time she opened the journal she wrote about their trip to Padre Island. By the time she opened the journal for the tenth time, Margie was writing letters to Daniel.

Dear D,

I had a wonderful Christmas. I hope you did, too. My younger brother, Mark, and his wife made the trip to Texas along with their little girl, Cindy. I'm an aunt now. Mom is doing poorly, strength wise that is.

She has to use a walker now, but her mind is as sharp as ever.

D did I ever tell you what a nice person you are? I don't mean the macho antics you pull when you're trying to be funny or clever. I mean, deep down inside. You'll make some woman very happy. I hope you've found her already.

I'm doing fine. My only regret is dropping out of school. But, I intend to finish. I'll have to see. I would certainly like to get a degree. I'll have to see.

I wish I knew where you are and what you're doing. I know we went our separate ways, but that doesn't mean you aren't on my mind. I hope you're having a good day. M

After the first of the year, Margie got a job at a

grocery store. It was a welcome diversion from the noise and boredom of the apartment. She met many of the townspeople. Some would chat with her, welcome her to the community, and wish her all the best. But the job soon became as tedious and uninteresting as binge watching reruns of Gunsmoke. She assumed, with a hint of irony, the reason many stores had gone to self-checkout was that anyone assigned to stand in one place and scan item after item for hours on end soon decided to quit.

Robert grew increasingly dissatisfied with his work, specifically the long hours, the apartment atmosphere, and Margie. She could sense it. His compliments became few and far between. She began to feel like a roommate instead of a wife. Their infrequent romps between the sheets were as passionate as ever, but Robert was as self-serving as other men she'd met in her life. Sexual climax for Robert was a signal to go to sleep. Margie longed to be held, to cuddle, to bask in the afterglow of their union. Instead, she was left naked and untouched lying on her side of the bed. She knew Robert was out like a light at times like these. So, for the warmth and sensation of his touch, Margie would place her arm over his shoulder and snuggle her body against his back.

Margie was ambivalent about children. One day she wanted them; the next day she didn't. In truth, she knew she loved children. She would rather have them now, at least one boy and one girl. But the crying and all the noise she heard around the apartment complex was enough to make her take the pill for the rest of her child-bearing years. The squabbling between toddlers, the constant whimpering of the dirty diaper brigade, the yelling of frustrated mothers. No wonder Mother Nature instilled a powerful drive in humans to procreate. Left to their own choices, significantly fewer would accept the responsibility. Margie was not on the pill. She knew the blessing of an infant was the result of timing, chance, and fortune. If a child were destined to bless her home, she would take it whenever it arrived, whatever the sex, whatever its condition. Mother Nature hadn't forgotten to instill the love and care mothers provide when it comes to raising babies.

Robert and Margie didn't renew their lease at the end of six months and moved into another apartment complex. The cars in the lot looked newer, cleaner. The carpet in their unit looked newer, cleaner. But they had little furniture of their own–a couch, a dinette set, and a bed and a dresser they both tried to use.

As they sat around the kitchen table one evening soon after they moved Robert said, "go and buy some furniture. This place looks like a cave."

Okay, hon. What do you want?"

"A TV bureau, or whatever you call it. Christ, that dinky TV we had at the other place. . ." He batted his hand through the air. Get a bigger TV and some chairs and a damned dresser where I can put my stuff."

"Okay, Robert, but you don't have to talk like that."

"Alright, alright." He rubbed his chin and jaw. Then he reached across the table and touched her arm. "Maybe you can find something more interesting to do on this side of town."

"I saw an ad for daycare providers at a nearby nursery and pre-school," she said.

Robert closed his eyes and nodded his head as a thought reached him and he smiled. "Yes, Margie. You might as well get some practice at it." When he opened his eyes, Margie was smiling too.

"I should probably get a bassinet, too."

"Are you pregnant?"

"No, no, no honey. Not yet. But I'd like to be."

CHAPTER ELEVEN

At the end of police academy training, Daniel stood in line decked out in a brand-new blue uniform, saluted the captain and received his commission. He was now one of Dallas' finest.

He was put on patrol with a salty veteran named Trammel. The man was pushing fifty with twenty-four years on the force, had a streetwise PhD in human psychology, and knew the layout of his beat better than Google maps.

"Never, ever take a situation as routine," he admonished. "The most mundane encounter with a citizen can turn into holy hell if you don't maintain awareness. Give every person respect and let them give their side of the story. But if you sense double-talk, you've probably got a situation where there's more to it than meets the eye."

When it came to coffee breaks, Trammel was

always on time. He could have been a poster child for donut shops across the country. He had a way of talking about nothing, then he'd look Daniel straight in the eyes, get real serious, and impart a nugget of policy wisdom.

"Right now, police across the country have a bad rap. The anarchists and trouble-makers have to have a scapegoat for their perceived injustices, so they blame the cops for society's ills. The truth is, it isn't bigoted cops that cause problems—it's a few cops with poor judgment. Anyone with a working brain cell knows one bad apple doesn't spoil the whole barrel. But these ingrates' sole purpose in life is to create distrust, animosity, and suspicion.

"Problem is, of course, it makes it harder for us to do our job. Don't get paranoid, but keep your head on a swivel. Safety first. There are too many crackpots out there who'll take a shot at you just because you wear a badge."

"You mean they'll fire on a cop just because they see a uniform?"

"Yeah, some people are that stupid, but what I'm driving at is when you've confronted them about something else. Reflex action. You'll encounter desperate people. They think they're going to get away with it, but it goes very bad for them."

Trammel ate the rest of his donut, then continued.

"But nowadays, you also have the smart alecs. They have the misconception they can be rude or confrontational with police. The bottom line is, if they don't comply with your lawful requests, they go to jail. If they want to give all their money to bail bond agents or lawyers, be my guest. Many of them think they can go to court and plead their own case. But even if the judge grants probation, it's still a conviction on their record. If they want a dismissal, they're going to need a lawyer, and we're talking upward of $1,000 for a lawyer to even show up at the courthouse. I don't think too many of them want to go through that more than once. But there's a lot of jerks who will test the system the first time around."

Daniel rode with Trammel for six weeks. Then he was paired up with an officer named Garrison. He was pushing thirty, an ex football player who played his college ball in Kansas. They hit it off, it seemed like a good fit. For starters, Garrison did the talking, Daniel served as backup.

But in the mornings, after his night shift, Daniel pined over his lost love. He seldom got to sleep before noon. Letters to her mother were returned, unopened. He couldn't envision a satisfactory explanation for her sudden departure. The guy she married must have hypnotized her. He racked his brain for an answer to 'Why.'

He would still feel empty, but at least he could understand if he'd hit her, or berated her, or used her as an object of cruel jokes. But he did none of that. He caressed her, kissed her, told her she was beautiful and the smartest girl he'd ever met.

At times his job was extremely difficult, but it kept his mind off of Margie. In that regard, it was a perfect occupation. In a six month period, he and Garrison recovered more stolen cars than any other team in the precinct. It crossed Daniel's mind that the insurance companies should pay a bonus for recovered vehicles. Yes, it was a criminal act and the perpetrators would be punished, but why should taxpayers foot the entire bill when the vehicles recovered saved profitable businesses thousands of dollars?

Shoplifters, he quickly surmised, were nothing but losers with sticky fingers. They would scream and kick until they were cuffed, then whine about how broke they were, on the doorstep of starvation, even when their theft was beer and cigarettes. Two adult women even tried that line when caught with $200 dresses in their underwear. They were going to sell the dresses in order to buy food for their children.

Then one night, one of many endless nights, Daniel and Garrison were called to a domestic disturbance. It resulted in an investigation that would change Daniel's life. He had been on similar calls, but often the offending party had fled the scene. Other times, the parties were in a state of reconciliation even though the man involved was ordered to go elsewhere to spend the night.

But tonight, Heath and Donna Diebold were on their lit porch while Heath took a leather strap to her for everyone to see. Even before the police cruiser stopped, Daniel could see not even a man could stand a beating like that.

Daniel was instantly out of the car ahead of Garrison and ran toward the house.

"Stop, police!"

Heath only flinched and whipped the belt across her back.

Daniel grabbed his baton and hit Heath across the hip. He cried out, dropped the strap, and ran. Daniel sprang to cut him off, dropped him in a jarring tackle, and cuffed him. All the while, Heath screamed obscenities and self-serving crap about his home and privacy. Heath appeared to be in his late twenties. His hair looked like it hadn't been washed in a month, and his scraggly facial hair looked about the same. He was lean and wiry but Daniel had him well in hand. Daniel pushed him toward the cruiser, and pushed Heath's cuffed hands up his back. Heath ceased his profanity-laced tirade and began screaming in agonizing wails of pain.

Donna lay unconscious on the porch. Garrison had called for an ambulance. She was breathing and wasn't bleeding. But her face was swollen to the point of being unrecognizable. Garrison held her arm and checked her pulse.

As Daniel walked back toward the house, the surroundings, for a moment, felt peaceful. No yelling and screaming going on. But a rage began to boil in him as he saw Donna's beaten body. She was a heavy set young woman, probably the same age as Heath. Daniel wondered how many beatings she had endured? And then he heard the crying. Garrison heard it too.

Daniel entered the house. There was a front room, eating area, then kitchen, front to back. The bedroom and bathroom were obviously off to the side. And there, huddled together under a lamp in the front room was a little boy and a little girl.

CHAPTER TWELVE

As soon as he saw them, Daniel stopped. The boy was on his knees, his eyes wide, searching Daniel's expression for any hint of what was to come. His shoulders and neck were tense. He seemed afraid but not terrified.

"How old are you?"

"Eight." The word was spoken as forcefully as the boy could muster. It sounded like a threat, a declaration he would defend the little girl beside him at all cost.

"You're going to be alright," Daniel said.

The boy's expression seemed to slacken, obvious pent-up emotion ready to give way.

The little girl knelt behind the boy. She held loosely to his shirt. She never looked up, but Daniel could tell she was listening intently.

"And how old is she?"

"She'll be five."

"You know I'm a policeman. I won't hurt you. I'm here to help."

"Will my mom be okay?" The words exploded from his lips. His face contorted as he tried to contain his emotion. He wasn't in tears yet, but they were barely held back by a dam of determination.

"Your mom will get the best of care." Daniel knelt on the floor next to them. "Your dad will be with us for a while. You and your sister will have a warm place to sleep."

"You won't let dad come back will you?" The question was a plea and the little fellow broke down. The silence he had forced upon himself while he listened to another beating his mother endured, finally gave way. Tears spilled down his face while he hugged his little sister.

"Don't let him come back, mister. Don't let him ever come back."

The little guy's sobbing brought Daniel to a cavern of human sorrow. He didn't show it, but the kid's anguish after witnessing another brawl between his parents was more than any feeling adult could stand. The little girl got up on her knees and hugged the boy around the neck. Garrison stood at the door. Sirens could be heard approaching in the distance. At that moment, Daniel vowed he would see these two children asleep in warm beds before he called it a night.

The woman had suffered a beating designed to inflict maximum pain without causing permanent injuries. But the husband may have gone too far. Presently, the woman was unconscious, but the ambulance was only minutes away. Garrison could handle that. Daniel would stay with the children.

What he wanted to know most of all was how Child Protective Services handled situations like this. What and where were Dallas' facilities for emergency children's care? Where was the women's shelter?. How big a problem was domestic violence? If a man couldn't treat a woman with love and affection, Daniel thought, he could at least keep peace in the home.

Sometime later, when the ambulance had come and gone, the representative from Children's Protective Services showed up. She was an older woman, certainly knew her authority and obligations for children under her care. She met the children and asked their names–Colton and Morgan. Then she questioned Daniel with a fact-finding list as though she were preparing to buy a horse. She was both assertive and impatient. Daniel got the distinct impression she had been pulled from reading the latest romance novel, and her rush to get the children packed into her car set Daniel on edge.

"Mame, where do you take children under these circumstances?"

"Oh, officer, I'm sorry, but that's confidential."

"What? Confidential, why? I know who they are, I know where they live, their parents."

"Policy."

The woman's condescending responses and business-like attitude around two small, helpless children pushed Daniel the wrong way. "Did we interrupt your evening?"

The woman caught the sarcasm. She stopped her writing and looked directly at Daniel. "Officer, these children will be well taken care of. The county does have accommodations and staff for these situations. Don't get riled up with me. I'm doing my job."

"I want to see these children in the morning–see how they're doing. I imagine the boy goes to school."

"I don't see how that can happen."

"Well then, who do I see to get permission?"

"The department director. If you want to be helpful now, see if they have jackets and a bag for extra clothes."

Immediately, the boy moved to the task while the little girl followed quickly behind him.

"Listen officer." The woman adopted a conciliatory tone and dropped her clipboard to her side. "I know these situations are very emotional. I understand your concern. But let me take care of the children. I will do exactly that. If you've separated the adults, you've done your job. There are no easy answers to these matters."

And for the first time since he found the children, Daniel took a deep, invigorating breath. She was right. This was the most exhausting call he'd been on during his short stint on the force.

"Okay, thank you." He helped the woman get the children into her car, and watched them drive away.

When Daniel and Garrison got back in the squad car, Daniel refocused his thinking on Mr. Heath Diebold as he drove to the city jail. What a piece of scum. It didn't matter to Daniel the kind of childhood Heath had experienced. He was a grown man. He had children. He had made a vow to a woman to honor and cherish. Maybe Donna was a mouthy bitch who started their rows until she was overcome by Heath's violence. It didn't matter. Heath was a loose cannon, predisposed to criminal violence, and Daniel's brain began to hatch a scheme to dispense true justice.

Daniel's mind spun multiple scenarios as he drove downtown. He would make every man guilty of domestic violence he came across pay for their sins. If the justice system wanted to coddle these reprobates, he would make them fully aware that their transgressions deserved a punishment worse than a few days in jail. When he saw the faces of that little boy and girl in his mind's eye, a righteous rage pulsed through him. How could anyone put such precious, innocent children through such emotional trauma?

Daniel imagined delivering the same justice to the man who had stolen his girl, though he didn't even know the man's name–yet. His mind floated to an image of Margie. What would she be doing this coming day? A New Year had come, the months slipped by like a stream over a spillway. Did Margie have a job or did she stay at home? Had she enrolled at another college?

He knew he was impulsive, possessive, an intellectual equivalent of a stalker. But he hadn't done anything. His anger, his remorse, his scheming were all internal. Most likely, he would never see her again. And yet, the unconscious mind works in silence behind the scenes. His wounded ego had found an outlet for his disappointment and damaged pride. The men who would feel the wrath of his hand would never know what hit them. Their pain would soothe Daniel's wounded soul. Daniel fully understood the displaced aggression he was contemplating. What he was considering was well outside the law, but his psyche needed the physical exertion of beating someone to a pulp. How truly justified it would be to dispense pain to men who themselves had dealt violence to others? The more he thought about it, the more it seemed right. And it would ease his mind.

But as much as he wanted an outlet for his anxiety and stress the thought would have never occurred to him if he hadn't seen the children. How many others had to cower and hide from a man who was supposed to care for them? How many boys were being shown the way to treat a woman? The very thought of all the vulnerable children had Daniel seething inside.

At Heath's arraignment, he was charged with first degree assault. He was unable to post bond. Donna had a broken jaw, three broken ribs, and welts over 80% of her body. Daniel would gladly testify at his trial. Heath was looking at several years in the state pen. Daniel could forget about Heath. The justice system had a firm grasp on him. But he couldn't forget the children.

CHAPTER THIRTEEN

In the weeks that followed, Daniel got a detective named Kulbiski to let him look at the recent case files of domestic violence. There was nothing improper about the request. The detectives could always use the assistance of patrol officers' eyes and ears. Some wanted abusers were still at-large. Daniel read each file meticulously. He wanted names and addresses. He couldn't believe the scope of the problem.

Daniel learned that Colton and Morgan Diebold had been placed in a foster home. At least they were together. Now he was intrigued with the workings of the foster care system. He may be able to locate them. He wanted to see them again. If nothing else to let them know the policeman who was there that horrible night cared about them.

But still, after two years on the force, when all the surprises, excitement, and paperwork of his night shift ended, Daniel lay awake on his apartment couch and thought about Margie. Nowadays, it increasingly crossed his mind that Margie never seriously cared about him at all. Maybe she just liked to tell her friends she was dating a football player. Or maybe Margie was fond of him in the beginning and their relationship had deteriorated without him being aware.

Maybe she had been seeing this guy she married all along. He didn't want to distrust women. He wanted to find a young woman and get married, but somehow he felt duped. Still, he couldn't blame Margie. He loved her too much. His wrath fell on the unnamed interloper, a man who ruined a meaningful relationship. There was a man out there who was a destroyer, no better than men who physically hurt their wives. Once Daniel went to his bedroom, it was an hour or more of fit-filled, disjointed dreams before he ever fell asleep.

I would rather cry about you,

than forget you.

Monica Collins

Daniel contrived no specific plan to confront wife beaters. Most were probably cowards at heart. But he knew he couldn't take any action wearing his uniform or in any official capacity. It would all be *mano y mano.*

Daniel's first encounter occurred almost by accident. He had left the house at 3 p.m. His police shift didn't begin until eight. He had an address not three miles from his location, and decided to drive by and see what kind of place it was. The neighborhood was a string of rundown, wooden, one car garage hovels. The curb was full of trash as far as he could see. He pulled his car over and studied the house. There were two cars in the drive, one up on blocks. If the front yard had any grass growing it was hiding under a beer can.

Daniel was about to drive on when the front door flew open, the screen door slammed against the house and a skinny woman scrambled across the sagging porch.

"Don't you ever come back, you conniving bitch," screamed a man who was on her tail. He threw something at her, but missed. He was as skinny as the woman. From what Daniel could see he didn't look older than thirty, but he had the sunken face of a man who didn't have a tooth left in his mouth. Daniel's cop instincts kicked in, but he waited. Sure enough, instead of letting her go, the man chased her down.

He grabbed her by the hair and proceeded to pull her toward the house. Daniel slipped out of his car, used the cars in the drive as cover, and was right behind the two when they made it back into the house. In fact, Daniel shut the door behind them. He didn't hear any other voices or commotion. They were a gathering of three.

The man resembled Heath Diebold so much that Daniel's body had already shifted into third gear by the time the man let the woman go and turned to face him. "Who in the hell are you?"

"The Avon lady. You have time to look at samples?"

The man's brain did a double take, but a split second later he was all piss and vinegar. "Get out of my house." Daniel saw the woman crawl into a bedroom. The man came forward and Daniel clocked him with a left hook that knocked the man against a dinette table and put out his lights. One punch and the wiry creep dropped like a dirty sock. Daniel didn't wait around for explanations. He didn't care what the woman's troubles were. He had accomplished the reason he got out of his car, and he did an about face and went back to it.

He knew he'd gotten the idea to mete out retribution to wife beaters when he saw what Heath Diebold had done to his wife. But it wasn't until this chance encounter he actually got the drive and nerve to dish out vigilante justice to strangers whose crimes he hadn't personally witnessed. After he'd slapped around a few more deadbeats, the urge grew to do it again. The confrontations became cathartic, exhilarating, additive. He was dispensing justice where the system had fallen short.

The vision of Colton and Morgan cowering under a lamp with their mother unconscious on the porch was a vision he could not tolerate. These unpredictable men weren't under undue duress. Their tantrums didn't spawn from the irrational demands of a hated boss. Debt collectors weren't banging on their door. These men could contribute to the peace and stability of their homes. Instead, they were as infantile as toddlers in the candy aisle. If the least little thing didn't suit them, they recklessly upset the entire family, often breaking things or hitting people they supposedly loved.

A few weeks later, another man's rap sheet caught his attention while researching the detective's files. The guy's name was Salem, age forty-one. He'd been arrested three times for domestic battery and convicted once where he'd spent six months at county. Salem's jail time was the result of a child endangerment charge. He'd thrown his wife on the floor and the woman landed on their two-year-old daughter. The child suffered a broken leg and significant bruises.

Salem lost custody of his three children, and according to the file, the woman had taken the children and moved out-of-state. Supposedly, he now lived alone in the Pleasant Grove area of Dallas. Daniel hoped to find the man alone.

At 6 P.M. on a Tuesday, Daniel parked his car two doors down from the address he intended to visit. He wore a light blue, long sleeved shirt pulled down as far as possible over blue disposable gloves, blue pants and a white ball cap. He appeared like an official currier at first glance. He carried a small package to the door. It was answered quickly after two knocks.

"Mr. Salem?"

"What is it?"

"A package for you, sir. You'll need to sign." The guy still had on his mechanics shirt from some dealership.

"What the hell. I don't sign for nothing. Who's it from?"

Daniel handed him the package with the fictitious return address. Within two seconds of Salem studying the address, Daniel tazed him with a shot to the neck. Salem yelped once and fell flat on the floor. Daniel jumped inside, pushed the man's legs out of the way and shut the door.

Salem groaned and writhed on the filthy shag carpet. "What do you want?" he pleaded as he tried to push himself up from his awkward position. Daniel rolled his fingers into a fist and cracked him in the side of the head.

Daniel pulled Salem's arms behind his back and cuffed him with plastic restraints. Salem was almost as big as Daniel, but Daniel was able to lift him and throw Salem over the back of a couch. Salem's face stuck in a front cushion while his toes dangled just above the floor. Daniel pulled the man's belt from the loops and pulled his pants down, underwear and all, until his white ass was in full view. Daniel proceeded to use the belt to inflict about thirty whacks on Salem's bare butt.

Salem screamed in agony.

When finished, Daniel leaned toward Salem's ear. "You're worthless scum. You deserve to be whipped. And keep this in mind, you call the cops and we'll come back and kill you."

Daniel liked the idea of making it sound like he was one of many. He had two hours before his shift began. He was ready for a productive night on the job. If he ran into anyone who wanted to challenge authority or play games with one of Dallas' finest that night, they'd be dealing with a cop who was locked and loaded.

Chapter Fourteen

The internet was a godsend when you wanted to find someone. The detectives at the station used it regularly. Easily tapped into vital statistics offices throughout the nation, many data companies now accessed the chain of individual's addresses.

It had been over two years since he'd seen Laura at the game. But he remembered the date of the game, and Laura said she had gotten married 'two weeks ago.' Daniel searched the marriage records of Tom Green County, Texas, for the week in question. And, there it was--Robert Rucker and Margaret Winters–attested by–presiding minister. His eyes glazed over. "Robert Rucker," he said. He let the name roll off his tongue. Such a strange sound. Who was this guy?

Daniel had a fleeting interest in whether the guy was actually a Marine. But, U.S. military records couldn't be accessed by private database companies. His only interest in the man was why Margie had chosen him over himself. She must have been drugged or blackmailed. Really? A high school fling that resurfaces and Margie jumps on his horse and rides with him into the sunset?

The continual rehashing, reliving, and questioning himself was like a splinter in his brain that couldn't be reached. Daniel closed his eyes and wiped away the tears. He was a commissioned police officer. On almost a daily basis, he saw the depths of human depravity, the violence, the cowardly acts, the deceit and lies. In spite of the suffering he saw or the reprehensible acts to one person committed by another, Daniel kept his poise and professional demeanor. But when he thought of Margie, his stoic facade melted like an ice cream cone in the sun and he felt weak and alone. The mental vision of Margie always brought on the tears. His only balm of consolation were the memories. No one could steal those away.

By the end of 1991, Robert Rucker had had enough of building roads. The constant standing and bending were bad enough, but the heat. How does a person catch their breath when standing on open ground that feels like an inferno? Robert worked a couple of hours every night submitting applications to every job vacancy he read or heard about.

Margie was now pregnant and to the point where she could no longer work at the daycare center. But they wouldn't move until after the birth. She had a local doctor. The blessed event could happen any day.

Robert got a response to his application from a car dealership in the town of Spinler, 100 miles away. The owner was an ex-Marine himself. Robert drove in on a Saturday to an interview. The owner didn't care what Robert knew about the auto parts business. Robert was young, married, articulate, and most importantly, an ex-Marine. He could be trained.

"When is the baby due?" asked the owner.

"This month," Robert replied. "Could be born this weekend. We're just waiting for the moment."

"Very well. I'll have someone check on apartment vacancies. We'll put up your deposit so you'll have a place to move into immediately."

"Thank you, sir." Robert stood and shook the man's hand. "This really is a nice little town."

"Yes, little being the keyword." The owner smiled. "But we sell trucks all over the county and beyond. People around here like to buy local and trade local."

Robert left the showroom ecstatic, ready to tell Margie the good news. He had secured a new job, and they'd be moving to the nice, quaint and quiet Texas town called Spinler.

Daniel and Garrison answered another domestic disturbance call that was easily de-escalated. An estranged brother had tried to get his sister to let him spend the night. He was drunk and she knew his M.O. A night's sleep would lead to breakfast, and then the man would lay about the house, pilfer what he thought was valuable, and never leave until physically dragged away. Daniel and Garrison gave him a personal escort to the Lew Sterrett Justice Center.

CHAPTER FIFTEEN

Officer Daniel King learned the two Dibold children had been placed with a couple named Franklin. Daniel called them, talked to Mrs. Franklin, and asked if he could see the children. She quickly agreed. He arrived in the evening.

Mrs. Franklin was a matronly woman, a bit of a waddle in her giddy-up, with red dishpan hands. She met him at the door with a warm smile. She seemed the type of woman who took life as it came, chores were a constant, a cheery disposition was the best tonic to ward off the melancholy of routine existence. Mr. Franklin was a carpenter, she explained, and still at work.

The Franklin's had taken in an older girl of thirteen named Becky who had been with them for two years. Daniel met her briefly in the living room. She acted quite demure and reserved, though she was quite pretty, in the full bloom of puberty. She introduced herself then moved to the kitchen.

The Franklin's had a son of their own, a boy named Bradley, a year older than Colton. He did not come out of the room the boys shared. Morgan was eager to see him and met him at the door. As soon as he stepped into the house, she hugged him around the knees.

"May I pick you up?" he asked.

Morgan raised her arms and Daniel pulled her up to his chest. She said nothing, but her face beamed with excitement. Morgan touched the rim of his cap and rubbed the metal insignia on his collar.

"Where's your brother?"

"In his room, I think," she said. "I can get him."

He let her down. "Tell him I'm here."

Colton appeared from the hallway, stoic, seemingly bored, as though the caller had done him no favors and he'd be pleased if Daniel left.

"Hello, Colton. Not even a handshake?"

"Don't you have a bank robber to catch?"

"Not right now. I caught them all this morning." The attempt at levity didn't budge the boy an inch. "So, how are you doing?" Daniel asked.

"We're here," Colton said as he threw open his hands in a jester of resignation.

"I'm here to help, Colton. I could probably take you to see your mother."

Mention of his mother, hit a nerve. "And what? Look at her lying in a coma. I don't want to see her like that. You're dumb."

Daniel smiled to himself, though the comment was well taken.

"So, where else would you like to go?"

"McDonalds," Morgan said.

Daniel went to the kitchen and talked to Mrs. Franklin. She agreed. Daniel promised to have them back in less than an hour. While Daniel ate a Big Mac the children went through their Happy Meals. Colton remained quiet and disinterested, while Morgan sat next to Daniel, obviously excited to sit close to a policeman. Nothing changed by the time they returned to the foster home. When Daniel drove away, he wondered if there wasn't something specific bothering Colton.

Clint Stocker moved back to the Memphis area after he graduated. Got married to Sara a month after he received his diploma just like he said. He called Daniel at least once every six months. He'd gotten Texas in his blood and he kept up with college classmates better than the chairman of the alumni association.

"Hey, Daniel, my friend. How's the world been treating you?"

"Absolutely fantastic. Everyone has decided to obey the law and I have nothing to do. My last arrest was two old ladies jaywalking."

"Ha! Hey, listen. A bunch of us are going deer hunting in east Texas around Longview. Have you ever been deer hunting?

"Yeah once, must have been a dozen guys. After freezing our asses off since before dawn, waiting in a blind, we met back up at base camp at ten. No one had gotten a thing except one trigger-happy joker killed Bambi. The little thing had barely lost its spots. We razed the hell out of the guy. "

"This will be better. You can have your deer butchered in town–venison steaks all cut and wrapped for your freezer. You have to come. Weekend of November 16th. Get back to me as soon as you can."

"I really don't know, Clint. I don't have any vacation time coming up."

"What the heck. You don't work seven days a week, do you?"

"Sometimes it feels like it."

"Make it work and get back to me. Talk to you later." With that, Clint hung up.

Daniel liked Clint, his phone calls, his stories, his updates on old classmates. He didn't even mind the idea of spending a weekend hiking through East Texas woods. But he didn't want to kill a deer, and he didn't want to see a dead one either. He got enough gunplay, injuries, and death in his work. He hadn't killed anyone himself, but he had drawn his sidearm a number of times. He'd seen the depravity of the human mind where life wasn't worth a dollar and the passion of emotion trumped common sense every time. He would never forget the day he saw a man shot to death in broad daylight. It turned out some wino shot his friend in the head because he wouldn't share his pint of gin. Daniel called Clint back and bowed out of the hunting trip.

I will always hold a candle for you,

even until it burns my hand.

Ranata Suzuki

CHAPTER SIXTEEN

Margie delivered a baby girl at the Fredericksburg hospital. Robert could force himself no further than the waiting room. He paced and worried. He dreaded the possibility of complications and knew he'd be distraught, bordering on revulsion, if the child had some physical deformity. When the nurse gave him the 'all-clear' he was more relieved than happy. They named the little girl Marie. Two weeks later, they moved to Spinler.

They had been married less than two years, and Margie realized Robert was bored with the routine of married life. Maybe he longed for the discipline, spit and polish, and potential excitement offered by the military. On numerous occasions she tried to discuss his lethargic attitude. If he had his choice what would he rather be doing? He was always too sullen to discuss it. He'd even given her dirty looks for her audacity to pry. Almost daily he grew more distant. It was as if he'd completed his required man's 'to-do' list–completed his basic education, served his country, gotten married and fathered a baby, and had a job. Was he going to coast downhill for the rest of his life?

But as they moved into their new home, Margie basked in the love of motherhood. The baby was a full time job, and she would have had it no other way. If Marie hadn't demanded almost constant care and attention, Margie would have been disappointed. As she and Robert grew apart, Margie showered her abundant love on her baby daughter. And when Robert fell into his chair in front of a televised college basketball game, Margie would sit on the porch and sing to Marie.

Robert took to his job in the parts department at the Ford dealership predominantly because he was out of the constant glare of the sun. He subscribed to a half dozen car magazines, in part, because it helped him learn his business. Then he began to fancy himself as a race car driver though he'd never even raced so much as a go-cart. Robert got the NASCAR bug. So, when the winter season of basketball was over there was always a car race to watch on the weekends throughout the spring and summer.

Robert and Margie kept in touch with relatives. Most lived around San Angelo. A grandchild must be cuddled and spoiled. Robert didn't mind trips of that kind every once in a while. Margie noticed he was satisfied to stay close to Spinler. He'd made friends with guys in the shop. They were all car buffs, but several had restoration projects going. Robert was invited to listen and learn and he spent hours at the different shops doing just that. Margie sighed and looked up at the evening sky. She could not believe the silent solitude she lived in was the replacement for the happiness she had dreamed.

After three years in the trenches with the dregs of society, Daniel sensed the growing callousness that coated his interactions with citizens. All he wanted to do was catch the perpetrators if they were on-scene, take down witness statements and be on his way. Let the detectives solve the cases. If he had to call an ambulance, he would do so. If he had to hold a crying baby, he could manage that as well. But he cared less and less for other people's problems. He had problems of his own. His biggest problem was that he couldn't forget.

Daniel kept the data research service. He checked it every week, if not every day. All he had to go by was the last name–Rucker.

A San Angelo address. Could they be living there? Laura said they moved, but she could have lied. Then, one day, an additional address popped up next to the one in San Angelo.

622 Sycamore Lane
Spinler, Texas

Daniel quickly looked up the town on the map–Spinler, Texas. He'd never heard of it. There it was, deep in the heart of the state. Land of sandstone cliffs, prairie grass, and Mesquite trees, Texas's contribution to large bushes. When he checked the town's population, Daniel burst out in laughter.

Spinler was a town of 3,000. What did it have? A filling station, a grocery store, and a grain elevator. Maybe a pharmacy if they were lucky. The mental image had him rolling on his carpet. Margie had said she wanted to get out of San Angelo. It was too small for her. So the yokel who marries her, drags her off to some bump in the road.

Daniel rehashed the information and was happier than he'd been in months. It was also unbelievable. Margie wouldn't stand to be sequestered in a town where the only entertainment was the occasional rodeo. Daniel knew Margie was too young and ambitious to drive down a Main Street where all the buildings were built a hundred years ago, and half of them now boarded and empty.

Or maybe she left Rucker and he went to Spinler to lick his wounds. Maybe Margie was still in San Angelo. But then, the pressure of pessimism crept into his thinking. The address in Spinler may belong to another Robert Rucker. The new address meant nothing to him now, and he lay on his couch and fitfully tried to fall asleep.

Daniel had an excellent psychological make up for being a cop. Confronting someone or making a traffic stop didn't raise his blood pressure a single point. He was neither excited nor apprehensive about such contacts. He did it by the book, polite and respectful. But he didn't play word games or coddle people who didn't obey instructions. Nevertheless, he didn't want to injure someone who was high on drugs, mentally ill, or even hard-of-hearing. If he ever had to fire his weapon, he would aim for the legs. He didn't want to kill someone. Whenever situations got heated, he made sure there was nearby cover for himself, and that he thoroughly assessed the situation.

The pressure relieving, physical exertion of kicking a deadbeat's ass, he knew, gave him the ability to be calm and collected in his police work. They were workouts. The encounters kept him in shape. At times, Daniel felt privileged to be able to carry out his extracurricular chore. The confrontations lowered his stress level. And Daniel also knew, the thought of another man motivated his righteous rage. The man had no face, he had no first name. But the thought of him drove Daniel's retribution. Pity to the wife beater who fell in Daniel's sights.

But he had to be careful. He was now twenty-five and a powerful man. Daniel was sure he'd busted one guy's jaw. Some sort of report would undoubtedly be filed when he showed up for medical attention. He knew, however, he would never end his quest. Some of the police reports on domestic violence made him sick. Others could bring a grown man to tears. Daniel would like to line them all up and have them shot. Nowadays, he relished responding to domestic calls. He could gather his own information for a follow up visit. He knew he'd been spending too much time going through files in the detective's office. He didn't want someone to put two and two together.

Daniel went by the Franklins once a week to see the Diebold children. Sometimes it was just a 'hello, how are you?" and he'd soon leave. Other times, Daniel would take them to McDonald's. Colton finally divulged his problem. The problem was with Bradley, Franklin's own son. Bradley was ten, an inch taller, and twenty pounds heavier than Colton. Bradley didn't like sharing his bedroom with a little kid. Daniel promised to talk to the Franklins and see if they couldn't reduce Colton's stress.

Daniel saw another potential problem lurking in the Franklin home and he smiled to himself. Their other foster child was fourteen-year-old Becky, a budding blossom of femininity if there ever was one. Bradley had taken notice. Though he was too young to know what to do with Becky even if she let him kiss her, he was considering his options. With Becky constantly around to fill his daydreams and scramble his hormones, even in the fifth grade, Becky was Bradley's number one subject. Daniel knew, for the time being, peace would prevail. But if Becky were still in the house up to her eighteenth birthday, the Franklins would have to chain Bradley to his bedroom wall and padlock the door.

Donna Diebold was pronounced brain dead by the doctors. For months, she had been in a coma on life support. Her father, her only close relative, made the decision to pull the plug. Donna was thirty-two years old. She was cremated and her ashes given to her father. The children were not told at the time.

Heath was tried and convicted of second-degree homicide. He was sentenced to twenty-five years in the Texas Department of Corrections. The children had been in foster care for some time already. They would be in foster care for much, much longer.

CHAPTER SEVENTEEN

Daniel crossed paths with Brenda Kline during a police call. Two robbers had hidden in the bathrooms until after closing time and had caught her alone in the office. The robbers wore masks and tied her hands behind her, then tied her to a chair. One of them waved a gun in her face, but left her unharmed. They got away with an entire day's receipts. After a half hour of struggle, Brenda was able to reach the remote alarm button under her desk and call for help.

Two squad cars responded to the call, The four officers involved, including Daniel, surrounded the store, guns drawn. The back door was unlocked and Daniel stepped through, his pistol aimed down the corridor.

"Police. Drop any weapons and raise your hands. The place is surrounded." He heard a muffled cry coming from a side room. Daniel slowly approached the doorway and saw a woman, tied hands and feet with her mouth taped. Her eyes were full of fear as Daniel untied her, but relief and thankfulness registered on her face once she was free.

"Are you all right?" he asked.

"Oh my, I'm so glad you're here." She let out a huge sigh of pent-up air. It sounded as if she'd been holding her breath for an hour. Her face dripped with sweat. Daniel helped her to her feet with one arm around her shoulders. He felt her involuntary shudders. And as he helped her up, he also felt her labored breathing, much like the staccato breaths he'd felt from a woman he'd held while sitting on the grass those many years ago.

"I thought for sure they were going to kill me," she said as she rubbed her wrists.

"Recognize anyone?"

"Not that I can say."

"Not one of your employees or regular customers?"

She shook her head.

"So what did they look like?"

"Two young men," she said. She gave him the best rundown she could of their physical sizes and what they were wearing.

"Anything else missing?"

"No, I watched them. They took the money and ran."

"Sure you're alright?"

She nodded. "Thank you."

She still had her purse and keys. She locked the store and got into a black Ford Fiesta. Daniel and Garrison followed her a couple miles to an apartment complex and waited until she entered a second-floor apartment.

"Think she'll be okay?" Daniel asked.

"She didn't need EMS," Garrison said. "She probably won't get any sleep tonight, but I'd say she's alright."

As they resumed patrol, Daniel replayed her expression when he untied her. She had to be over thirty, that age where the girlish look finally fades. He noticed she wore no ring. Her blonde hair rested on her shoulders and she had dimples. She was a big gal, but Daniel didn't see her as fat. But she wasn't his type, so why was he assessing her physical attributes? He had a robbery to report on and he was thinking about another damsel in distress.

He liked Margie's petite body type instead, her quick wit, her smiling eyes. He wondered how this woman looked when she smiled. In that instant when their eyes met, Daniel saw something of interest. He was curious about her. In a day or two, he would approach her. He would ask how she was doing. He would try to say something funny to get her to smile.

He didn't understand why he tortured himself by comparing other women to Margie. Margie was no longer a debutante herself. She'd probably dropped a kid or two by now leaving her backside as wide as a horse trailer. Thoughts of her were episodes of anguish, plowing worn out ground that would never yield a crop, throwing a line in a pond when he knew good and well all the fish were gone.

Brenda Kline was in the back when he went to the pizza shop. She came out when he asked for her and took him to the back office.

"How are you doing? Thought I'd stop and check."

"I'm fine. Thanks for asking."

He remembered the animated terror in her eyes when she'd been tied up. There was none of that in her expression now. Her face was plain, yet serene. But Daniel saw intelligence in her bright blue eyes.

"Did the detective get back to you?"

"Yes, in fact he did. This morning. They caught the kids involved. Of course, we'll never see the money." She opened her hands with an air of defeat.

"At least you weren't hurt." A pause hung over the room. He stood at the doorway with his police cap in his hand, and he knew he was stalling.

"Was there anything else?" she asked as she sat back in her chair and waited patiently. "If you want a pizza, it's on the house." And a beautiful smile erupted on her otherwise plain countenance. She had known he was waiting on something and she broke the ice herself.

"No, no it's not pizza, but. . . would you like to go to a movie?"

She didn't balk or question. She sat forward and looked Daniel straight in the eye. "Yes, I'd love to go to a movie."

"How about tomorrow. I'm off then. I can pick you up at your apartment. I know where it is."

She looked closely at his name tag. "Okay, Officer King."

"Call me Daniel."

"Okay, Daniel. My name's Brenda."

"I'm glad you don't mind dating a police officer."

She smiled a pleasant, warm smile. "I don't mind at all."

The movie date was a success. After that, Daniel wanted to take her out for an evening on the town. Unfortunately, both of them were busy in the evenings, so every day for a month straight, he took her out to a late breakfast. They would sit and gaze over their cups of coffee and just look at each other. Brenda was not a looker. Several teeth were out of line. Her hair was blonde but it lacked body or shine as though it was never permed or curled. Daniel wondered how it would look gathered up in a ponytail or wrapped in a bun atop her head. Her nose was slightly large on an already broad face, but he already knew there was something valuable behind those pretty blue eyes.

Brenda was more than a woman happy to have been asked out by a man in uniform. She was observant and aware. He had no doubt, she could say no when necessary or intercede if a situation called for it. She was the middle child of seven–all girls. For fourteen years her mother had a child every two. She and her sisters now ranged in age from 27 to 39.

After a two-month courtship, they set a date to be married. All of her sisters would be bridesmaids. Her sister Judy would be her maid of honor.

The Kline's extended family stretched across Texas into both Oklahoma and Louisiana. There were so many grandchildren, cousins, aunts, uncles and friends from Brenda's side of the family the church sanctuary was packed. Daniel's family was there and old high school friends that lived nearby along with a number of officers from the precinct. Clint gladly accepted Daniel's request that he be his best man. Daniel was caught in a whirlwind of well-wishers and handshakes. Brenda's loving smile kept him grounded. The reception was a Kline family reunion, but Daniel and Brenda were still centers of attention. After all the music and dancing, cake and punch, first dances and bouquet toss, the happy couple headed for Galveston. When they arrived at their hotel, they were exhausted. The endless vista of the Gulf of Mexico loomed out their bedroom window. They fell asleep in each other's arms. When the morning sun glistened off the water and lit their room, they consummated their marriage.

CHAPTER EIGHTEEN

When Marie began pre-school, Margie went back to work. She swore off working at a grocery store in any capacity. She was hired at a farm and ranch store because she was familiar with animal feeds, bridles, gates, post hole diggers, and just about anything a farmer could need or want. She liked being out of the house and making her own money. And she politely deflected flirtatious young men who tried to get her to smile at their worn-out one-liners.

The town had enough young bucks who stayed in Spinler after high school to keep the single female population properly pursued. Margie wasn't interested in amateur advances and she kept her wedding ring distinctly in view.

Margie joined a book club that met every two weeks. There were twelve women in the group and one elderly gentleman. It was an opportunity to make friends and learn new things about the town. She found herself enjoying the way the women talked about recipes and newborn children as though they were the most exciting topics in the world. They never talked about politics or anything bad in the news. The books they read were discussed as though the characters were real and fully deserving of the praise or derision attributed to them by the author.

Second only to the diner, the local bowling alley was the town's meeting hall. With league bowling three nights a week the place was always active. Margie heard more laughter and saw more happy faces there than she ever witnessed in her home. Slowly, she met new people, made friends, and adjusted to life in a small town.

But life at home was drudgery. Margie now realized Robert was a narcissist. Once he made a conquest, attained a goal, got someone to accept his point of view, the game was over. After working relentlessly to get someone to accept his opinion on this or that, Robert looked down on that person thereafter. There was no life in the house, no humor, no affection. If it weren't for Marie, Margie would have fallen into depression.

In 1998, Margie became pregnant again. Ten weeks later she miscarried. She cried for days. She knew the stress of home life contributed to the personal tragedy. She wondered how Robert kept his job if he acted at work the way he did at home– sullen and demanding. And when he did get something he liked such as a lemon pie, he'd berate Marie for not eating all of her serving. If Margie received a thank you for taking the extra time to make him a pie, she couldn't remember.

After being around his mechanic buddies, Robert began smoking. Margie asked him to smoke outside, and for a while he did. But when he hit a pack a day. He bought an ashtray in the shape of a leaf, sat it on the arm of his recliner, and watched TV while he puffed away.

Margie wondered, what did Robert think adult and married life would be? He didn't learn a useful trade in the military. He didn't even attend college much less graduate with a degree in anything. His grumbling at home only increased over time. Where a normal man would express some appreciation for a home cooked hot meal, or his work clothes always ready in the closet, washed and pressed, Robert was silent. But let something twist his testicles the least little bit, and he'd whine and complain until he went to sleep. He and Margie now slept in separate beds. Their sexual exploits hadn't diminished in any significant way. Robert would carry Margie to his bed, kiss her passionately and whisper words of his undying devotion. When he was through, he'd get up, and wash up. Margie knew that was her signal to move. Robert liked to sleep alone.

Over time, Robert's voice grew louder. His displeasure and complaints erupted over the most trivial things–a bit of trash stuck to the garbage can under the liner, Marie leaving her colored pencils and drawing books on the den floor between his recliner and TV, Margie moving his cigarettes so Marie wouldn't get ahold of them.

Two months after her miscarriage, her mother

make friends and learn new things about the town. She found herself enjoying the way the women talked about recipes and newborn children as though they were the most exciting topics in the world. They never talked about politics or anything bad in the news. The books they read were discussed as though the characters were real and fully deserving of the praise or derision attributed to them by the author.

Second only to the diner, the local bowling alley was the town's meeting hall. With league bowling three nights a week the place was always active. Margie heard more laughter and saw more happy faces there than she ever witnessed in her home. Slowly, she met new people, made friends, and adjusted to life in a small town.

But life at home was drudgery. Margie now realized Robert was a narcissist. Once he made a conquest, attained a goal, got someone to accept his point of view, the game was over. After working relentlessly to get someone to accept his opinion on this or that, Robert looked down on that person thereafter. There was no life in the house, no humor, no affection. If it weren't for Marie, Margie would have fallen into depression.

In 1998, Margie became pregnant again. Ten weeks later she miscarried. She cried for days. She knew the stress of home life contributed to the personal tragedy. She wondered how Robert kept his job if he acted at work the way he did at home—sullen and demanding. And when he did get something he liked such as a lemon pie, he'd berate Marie for not eating all of her serving. If Margie received a thank you for taking the extra time to make him a pie, she couldn't remember.

After being around his mechanic buddies, Robert began smoking. Margie asked him to smoke outside, and for a while he did. But when he hit a pack a day. He bought an ashtray in the shape of a leaf, sat it on the arm of his recliner, and watched TV while he puffed away.

Margie wondered, what did Robert think adult and married life would be? He didn't learn a useful trade in the military. He didn't even attend college much less graduate with a degree in anything. His grumbling at home only increased over time. Where a normal man would express some appreciation for a home cooked hot meal, or his work clothes always ready in the closet, washed and pressed, Robert was silent. But let something twist his testicles the least little bit, and he'd whine and complain until he went to sleep. He and Margie now slept in separate beds. Their sexual exploits hadn't diminished in any significant way. Robert would carry Margie to his bed, kiss her passionately and whisper words of his undying devotion. When he was through, he'd get up, and wash up. Margie knew that was her signal to move. Robert liked to sleep alone.

Over time, Robert's voice grew louder. His displeasure and complaints erupted over the most trivial things–a bit of trash stuck to the garbage can under the liner, Marie leaving her colored pencils and drawing books on the den floor between his recliner and TV, Margie moving his cigarettes so Marie wouldn't get ahold of them.

Two months after her miscarriage, her mother

died. That night, as she read Marie a bedtime story, Margie wondered what she might have done differently to avoid being trapped in an unloving home, harnessed by a piece of legal paper, dismissed like a minimum wage housekeeper. Her brothers made funeral arrangements. She told Robert she'd take Marie with her to the funeral in San Angelo and she'd be back in several days. He nodded and lit another cigarette. "Drive safe."

CHAPTER NINETEEN

Brenda was proud of her police officer husband. Daniel was relieved and happy to come home to a woman. And could she cook. She knew a lot more about the culinary arts than just throwing toppings on pizza dough. Thoughts of Margie hadn't crossed his mind for weeks. Daniel moved into Brenda's apartment, but they soon bought a house in Garland, a suburb east of Dallas. Too often they had to sleep alone because of their schedules, but when they were together, Brenda always waited until Daniel came to bed. If he wanted sex, she was willing and passionate. If he didn't she would snuggle her cheek against his shoulder and tell him something good about the day, before they both fell off to sleep.

Brenda was thirty-three and desperate for children while she could still have them. Daniel wanted a family too. Unadulterated pride was the first emotion to hit him when she told him of her pregnancy a year after their marriage. But the last two months of her pregnancy were particularly difficult. Her blood pressure was unstable. The doctor put her on complete bed rest. During labor her blood pressure became dangerously high. She had to be rushed into surgery as her condition became a medical emergency and she received several transfusions due to massive blood loss.

But a healthy child was born. They named the little girl Melissa. It was the happiest and saddest day in the lives of both Daniel and Brenda. She would never be able to carry another fetus to term . Brenda and the baby spent five days in the hospital, but when they came home Daniel held Melissa and felt the pride of a first time father. He carried the baby over to her mother and sat beside them.

"You're going to be a wonderful mother, sweetheart," he said.

"Thank you, Daniel. She's healthy, everything we could ask for."

"Now we have a family."

Even in her happy moment, the comment caught Brenda the wrong way. "An only child. Oh, Daniel, I'm so sorry."

"Don't talk like that. She's beautiful. I'm happy. You're wonderful." And he kissed her.

Daniel was thankful he had met Brenda. He cared about her deeply. She was smart and caring with an engaging smile and bright blue eyes. But when Daniel made love to her, he had Margie on his mind. He was hurt by his emotional betrayal of

Brenda, but he couldn't help it. A man's heart can truly belong to one woman alone.

Daniel had a brain that compartmentalized his experiences. He didn't talk about his police work at home. He didn't talk about his family at work. He didn't talk about Margie at all, but the memories played in his head over and over just the same.

He wanted to know something about Margie. Why couldn't she be a singer or an actress? He could follow her life vicariously through her performances. An idea came to him. She may not actually live in Spinler, Texas, but then she might. He would subscribe to the town's newspaper. It was probably published weekly. He would read his copy from front to back. Small town newspapers pick up on all kinds of mundane town activities. Maybe her name would show up every once in a while.

As for the address he had for Margie in Spinler, he dismissed it. Writing her would never work. He wouldn't know how she took the correspondence. Would she throw it away as soon as she knew it was from him? Would she sit down and read it twice? Either way, he knew she would never write back. He could tell her he had saved a dozen lives in a daring hostage rescue and received a commendation medal from the city, and he would never know if she cared.

No–if he ever got the chance, got her number, got the nerve, he would contact her by phone. On the phone she would at least give him the chance to say hello. He smelled breakfast cooking. He now had a wife he adored, a child he loved unconditionally, and a home. He had to eat, then go to bed to get ready for another shift that began at 8 P.M. What was Margie doing today?

CHAPTER TWENTY

Demands of his job and obligations at home left Daniel with little time to reminisce about old romances. Yesterday, he and Garrison arrested a woman trying to fill forged prescriptions. Such encounters bored him. He'd heard the excuses before. The attempt was clearly illegal. But Daniel, in cases like these, wanted to give the perpetrator a swift kick in the butt and let them be on their way.

The job of the police force should be to deal with violent individuals in society. More than half of their calls were nuisance complaints such as someone finding someone else's car parked in their clearly designated spot. Or someone had a beef about an extra charge on their hotel bill. If it weren't so pathetic, it'd be laughable. So many citizens wouldn't give a cop the time of day, but let them get in the least little spat even children could resolve, and they're on the phone to the police.

Later in the day, he found himself at a house fire. The place was a goner, a gigantic bonfire, hot enough to be felt down the block. The fire trucks were there. No one was at home. He and Garrison got to play perimeter guards at the neighborhood spectacle. Daniel had already been to several and he knew–everyone thinks they want to see a house fire. Once you've seen one, you've seen them all. He had better things to do. If spectators got too close to a burning building, that's on them. Daniel looked about, he knew better. He wasn't upset by playing guard duty at a house fire. It was the constant sound in the back of his brain that wouldn't let him be completely happy and satisfied.

The days rolled by. Daily habits, reinforced by the necessity of routine, put his brain on autopilot. Yet, he never let his guard down. The mental preparation came with putting on his police uniform. At home, it was a kiss, a meal, he'd hold the baby for a while. This was the life he'd been given–not the one he would have chosen. But he knew better than to complain. It was a good life. His work made a difference. His work was indispensable to the community. His home life was good too. Brenda was a wonderful woman. He was full of smiles as he watched Melissa crawl across the floor.

But there were other days when his mind was wound tight. Some days his energy was extra high, bubbling, pulsing, thrown into overdrive. He could have chased several suspects, but he wasn't tired in the least. He could complete a full shift and still be on edge. It was as if he'd played a full football game that went into overtime, and he was as excited and rested as before the first snap.

Despite the danger, ignoring the risk, Daniel's mind and body were ready when he had another deadbeat in his sights. He knew their address, their place of work, and something about their schedule. If a picture was available, he studied it like a fingerprint.

Right after they got off work was a good time to catch them, although he had but an hour or two before his shift began. This time, after his night shift ended, he would wait until his target left for work in the morning.

Beyond the fact that his unlawful acts of retribution were stress relieving, Daniel didn't analyze the motivation behind his attacks. His targets were scum. They had beat up on their women because they were cowards at heart. That was his original determination. He found no need to consider it more. Daniel was in prime athletic condition. He had the size and strength to handle most men one on one.

Daniel waited two doors down in a crummy neighborhood off Ferguson Road. The entire street had overhanging trees begging to be pruned. The address he had for a Jimmy Dansler was a wooden pile of kindling that hadn't seen a paintbrush since the day it was built. A rusty Ford pickup sat in the drive.

A boy, around age twelve or so, came out and caught the school bus at 7:45. His jeans were frayed at the cuffs. His shirt looked like it had been worn everyday for a week. Daniel wondered how many times the boy had witnessed his father's rage or been a victim of it. Just the thought of children around these simmering volcanoes of unpredictable men built a rage within him. Daniel would wait. He wanted to see who else came out of the house. He waited until nine, and no one else exited. Daniel drove around the block, parked in another location, put on disposable plastic gloves, pulled his sleeves down as far as they would go, and walked to the door.

Daniel knocked on the door and was greeted by a man with a cigarette in one hand and a beer can in the other. He had on pants but was shoeless and bare chested. His hair was a ratted mass on his head and despite having had time to go to the refrigerator, appeared as if he had just gotten out of bed.

"Morning, sir," Daniel said. "Mr. Danmeyer?"

The man standing at his door and the question infused Jimmy's brain with a shot of oxygen and he gazed foggily at Daniel. "Who'd you say?"

"Well, I can't quite read it. It's a summons for Mr. Danmeyer to appear in court."

"What the hell? Well, my name is Dansler so you can take your paper and shove it up your ass."

In a microsecond, Daniel drew his Taser and shot the man in the chest. Beer went flying. The man hit the floor in a tangle of arms and legs. A soft moan blubbered from his lips. Daniel pulled him inside and shut the door.

A voice came from the bedroom. "Jimmy, who's there?"

Daniel quickly slipped wrist cuffs on Jimmy with his arms behind his back, then stepped to the bedroom where a woman was getting out of bed. Daniel watched from just outside the door as Jimmy's moans became louder. The woman rose from the bed with the speed of a sloth. Her efforts to combat her nocturnal stupor fought a losing battle. She held onto the bedpost as she reached for a cigarette. Daniel grabbed her from the back and covered her mouth.

"Don't make a sound or I'll cut you."

He could see black marks on her neck, but he looked for nothing more. He wanted to subdue the woman without hurting her.

"Don't look at me if you want to stay alive. Put your hands behind your back."

"Please don't hurt me," she wailed. She tried to turn and face him. Daniel grabbed her hair and pulled it back until she cried louder.

"Put your hands behind your back," he demanded.

She feebly complied. Daniel pushed her onto the bed with his knee in her back. He pulled off a pillowcase and pulled it over her head. He stuck a sock from the floor in her mouth and wrapped plastic cuffs around her feet. He left her face up on the bed, crying and moaning.

Back in the living room, Jimmy had rolled onto his back. His eyes were as wide as an owl's and just as unblinking. He wasn't a small man, but fat and out of shape. Daniel pulled Jimmy to his feet and cracked his forehead into Jimmy's nose. His nose instantly spewed a gush of blood. It was a bad move. Daniel had been so intent on giving this guy a beating he richly deserved that he got carried away and drew blood. Blood sprayed all over his shirt and hands.

"Whaddaya want?" Jimmy cried out, spewing more droplets of blood. He was terrified mostly because he didn't know why he was being attacked. Daniel found the confusion to work to his advantage.

Daniel kicked his leg from under him and dropped him on his front. "Who's the woman in the back?" Daniel asked.

"It's my wife." A clot had formed on his upper lip and he spit blood with every word.

"Not anymore. She's dead meat. You beat her up so often I just put her out of her misery."

A moan erupted from Jimmy's throat full of anguish and fear.

"I figure I'll just cut off your nuts and you won't be so violent. A little girlie boy."

"Oh my god. No, please no. I'll never . . . I'll never.

"Better get your pants down and get this over with."

"No, no don't." Jimmy fought to keep his belt and zipper from being reached. "Please, please. Don't do it."

Daniel unbuckled Jimmy's belt and pulled off his trousers. Then he took the knife to his boxers and cut them off. By now, Jimmy was rolling back and forth. Daniel put a knee in Jimmy's chest. "I'm not going to take them. You can put them in a jar and look at them whenever you want."

As Daniel rolled the knife in his hand, Jimmy was overcome with absolute terror. Daniel quickly took the loose belt and looped it around Kimmy's ankles, then stuck the filthy boxers in his mouth. He pulled Jimmy to the backdoor by his matted hair, threw open the door, and pushed him down the steps. Daniel washed his hands and face of dried blood as best he could in the kitchen sink, and stepped out the back door again, and kicked Jimmy in the side as he headed through an open field toward his car.

Daniel took off his shirt and stuck it under his car seat. He didn't have another shirt in the car so he drove to a consignment store and bought another. When he got home, Brenda had breakfast ready for him. She didn't ask why he was running late, but he saw her take a second look at the shirt. After all, he only had about ten dress shirts and she'd seen them all. She'd washed each one of them time and again. But if the new shirt posed a question to her, Brenda didn't say a word.

CHAPTER TWENTY-ONE

By the time Melissa began walking, Daniel had been visiting the Diebold children for years. Daniel thought about them, almost as much as he thought of Margie. Colton was almost twelve now, Morgan nearly nine. He wanted to do more for them. He wanted to do more for Brenda.

On one of their trips to McDonald's, Daniel drove them over to his house. He wanted them to meet Brenda. Morgan was the first through the door. She gazed about with an expression of adventure. She approached Brenda with unabashed confidence, and took her offered hand.

"Hi, I'm Brenda. I'm Mr. King's wife."

"Yes, I know." Morgan turned to the toddler and watched her with childlike fascination as Melissa walked along using the coffee table for support. She waited at the end of the table where the two little girls looked each other over. Morgan beamed a smile toward Brenda, an expression of delight of the child in front of her.

Colton walked into the house as though he were entering a cell. He was stoic and reserved. He obviously didn't like any hint of change, and was suspicious of anything outside his usual routine. He stood just inside the door, stiff as a fencepost and just as immovable. Brenda walked over to him.

"Hello, young man. I've heard a lot of good things about you."

Colton's rigid posture was almost comical. He looked at Brenda like she was a dried up, old aunt he didn't want to touch. His gaze was fierce and he communicated, in no uncertain terms, he'd be glad when the visit was over.

Daniel stepped inside and closed the door. He put his hand on Colton's shoulder. The boy pulled back and walked several paces away.

"See what I told you, dear. Smart and good looking pair. Colton here is just bashful."

"I'm not bashful."

"Cat got your tongue then. Or maybe you don't know how to introduce yourself to a lady."

Colton shot a stare Daniel's way that would have set a bush on fire. Colton remained silent.

"You don't need to be that way, Colton. She just wanted to meet you and your sister because I mentioned you after some of our visits. Are you always going to shut everyone out? I'd like to think my interest in your wellbeing has meaning to you. There are a lot of kids out there no one cares about."

Colton took a deep breath. His demeanor didn't change. He had the distinct expression of one who, when the speeches were over, would like to go.

"Listen." Brenda directed herself to Colton. "I know you were going to get something to eat. I've made sloppy joes. They're like hamburgers, but even better."

"I know what they are," Colton said.

Daniel and Brenda looked at each other and smiled though Daniel had a hint of resignation in his eyes. Would he ever get through to the boy?

Brenda led the way to the kitchen table. The children each ate two sandwiches and drank two tall glasses of milk.

Daniel picked up Melissa and helped her eat. Daniel smiled as he fed Melissa spoonfuls of sloppy joe meat. She was hungry and messy, but Daniel loved the experience. She was his baby. His child with Brenda, bright blue eyes, and the face of a cherub. Just holding her filled him with joy. Daily worries, problems on the job, and the agony of distant memories all faded with his little girl in his arms. He gave Melissa her sippy cup and watched her drink and kissed her on the cheek.

"Did that fill you up, Morgan?" Brenda asked.

Morgan nodded.

"That was good, Mrs. King," Colton replied.

"You're welcome, Colton"

Daniel kissed her as the children headed out the door. "I guess good old home cooking does the trick."

"You should know. You've certainly put on a pound or two."

"Thanks, dear. You're fantastic.

When they returned to the Franklin's house, Colton jumped out and ran inside. Morgan scooted across the seat and got to the ground. As she held the door she asked, "Mr. King, are we going to come live with you?"

Her question was not an idle request. She wanted to know, and Daniel knew the answer she wanted to hear. Out of the mouth of a child. Daniel felt the pang of uncertainty along with an infusion of hope.

"I don't know, honey. I don't know."

No one compares to you,

but there is no you,

except in my dreams

Lana Del Rey

CHAPTER TWENTY-TWO

One evening after supper, Daniel finally decided to talk to Brenda about something pressing on his mind. He thought it would be exactly what Brenda would want, but he didn't want to hurt her with unpleasant memories. She moved about the kitchen putting away leftovers.

"Honey, would you come sit with me? I have something to tell you."

Brenda wiped off her hands, then sat in their big living room chair as Daniel had already seated himself on the edge of the couch. Her eyes were bright. "What is it?" she asked. She smiled the caring, loving way she always did. She had a way of infusing light into any room. She was a woman of the highest caliber. If she wasn't taking care of Melissa and him, she was helping someone from the church.

"It's not any kind of news, dear. I wanted to talk to you. Get your opinion. See if this is something we want to do."

"Of course, Daniel. I'm open to anything you want to discuss."

"I've been thinking a lot about the Diebold children," he said.

"Yes."

"You know, they're not getting any younger. The Franklin's are nice people. You've never met them have you?

"No dear."

"You'd like Mrs. Franklin. Both of them are quite friendly but they have a houseful. I met Mr. Franklin once. He seems like a solid guy."

"Did you give him a 'get out of jail free' card?

Daniel perked up and gave her a smile. "No I didn't. I was all out that day. You're certainly in a bright mood tonight."

"Oh, you always put me in a good mood, dear, when you beat around the bush."

"Okay, yeah I was going to mention something to you."

"I'm listening, Daniel. I think it's probably a good idea."

Daniel nodded his head to confirm her affirmation. "I think we should adopt Colton and Morgan. There I said it."

And Brenda reached to him and pulled him to her breast and kissed him as passionately as she ever had. "I love you, Daniel King. You're a wonderful man."

Daniel hired an adoption lawyer who began the process. He and Brenda met with the children's social worker and a woman at Child Protective Services. There were no parents who had to consent to the adoption, the children were wards of the state of Texas. After the King's passed all background checks the matter was relegated to paperwork and within three months the process was completed and approved.

During that time, Daniel continued to visit the children, but he never let on anything was in the works. He didn't mention anything to the Franklins either, but the social worker informed him they had been advised. They would be sorry to see the children go, but would immediately be presented with other children who needed a foster home. There was no shortage of children in need as well as a substantial shortage of available homes like the Franklins.

On one visit Daniel had the children hop in his car. He was going to treat them to another meal of Brenda's home cooking.

Morgan was always excited to go anywhere with Daniel. "I want to see Melissa," she said.

"Melissa wants to see you, too. Would you like to be able to see her all the time?"

Morgan cocked her head in thought and blinked her bright brown eyes. "That would be nice." Her words were spoken slowly, as if attempting to reconcile how that would be possible.

Daniel pulled into his driveway. "I know Mrs. King is looking forward to seeing you. She has your favorite foods all prepared."

The living room was full of colored balloons and crepe paper bunting. Morgan's familiar enchanted expression beamed at the sight. Colton appeared quizzical. "Is it Melissa's birthday?" he asked.

"Let's eat first," Brenda encouraged as she hugged Morgan and graciously accepted Colton's offered handshake.

The table was set with sloppy joe sandwiches, tomato soup, breadsticks and plenty of milk. "We have apple pie for dessert," Brenda said.

"Is there going to be a party?" Morgan asked.

"Would you call it a party, dear?" Brenda said.

"That's kind of what I heard, hon," Daniel said, "some special people are coming over tonight and there's supposed to be a celebration."

"Oh boy," Morgan said between bites, "a celebration."

Instead of using the spoon, Colton drank the soup straight from the bowl. He set it down and looked at the two adults. "What are you talking about? You're just talking. Who's coming over?"

"Do you want more soup, Colton?" Brenda said.

"No." He dug into a sloppy joe.

When they finished eating, Daniel brought the children into the living room and sat them on the couch. Brenda sat in a chair beside the coffee table.

Daniel took Morgan's hand in his and faced the children. "Mrs. King and I thought you two might like to come and live here." He waited and watched as two innocent faces processed the information. The children's senses were on high alert. Neither of them said a word. They were listening for more.

"You could have your own room, Colton. You wouldn't have to share a room with Bradley anymore. And Morgan, you could see Melissa every day."

A gasp rushed from Morgan's throat. "Oh yes, yes."

Colton's expression was defensive. Whenever he had to deal with something new, his approach was always non-committal and questioning.

"Colton, would you like that?" Brenda asked.

He nodded the most lackluster, resigned acceptance to the idea he knew had already been finalized. Once again, his opinion held no weight. His body was again thrown into the air and left to land wherever adults wanted. Even good news he feared. Colton didn't like change–period.

Daniel and Brenda exchanged a glance and Brenda made the announcement.

"Colton and Morgan–we have adopted you."

Morgan's face flashed puzzlement and she looked at Colton and then Brenda.

"Sweetheart," Brenda said. "That means you are now part of this family. Mr. King and I are now your mother and father."

"Oh daddy," Morgan exclaimed, and she hugged his neck with all her might. "I knew you would do it. I knew you would. Oh, I'm so happy."

Colton remained pensive and perplexed as though the news had no real meaning. He understood the implications, but acted as though he could care less.

"You'll like it here, Colton," Brenda said as she patted him on the knee.

"We'll go back over tomorrow and you can get all your things," Daniel said. "For tonight, we have everything you need. Mrs. King, mother, will show you your new rooms."

DANIEL'S OBSESSION

CHAPTER TWENTY-THREE

Weeks passed, then months. Since they moved into the King home, Morgan and Colton each approached their new environs differently. Morgan became Melissa's big sister. Morgan was now nine, Melissa four. Morgan used the little girl as a make-up model. They had tea parties together. Brenda was delighted.

The adoption was final. As nice as the Franklins were, living with them had to be considered temporary, no matter how long the children were there. Colton and Morgan now had a home of their own. But Colton was as reserved and introverted as ever. He was polite to Brenda but hardly affectionate. With Daniel, he could be downright caustic. He never expressed appreciation for his new home and worked minimally at his schoolwork. His pent-up hostility and resentment remained bottled up, and Daniel was at a loss as to how to deal with it. Daniel took him bowling and to the rec center for pick-up games of volleyball. They made a few trips to the driving range. On their outings, the two got some exercise, but a breakthrough with Colton never came.

One evening, when Colton picked through his supper, his attitude characteristically sullen, Daniel walked into the kitchen dressed in his police uniform.

"Garrison's sick. I need you to ride along tonight and be my partner," Daniel said.

The unexpected quip brought a glint to Colton's eyes. His brain parceled the notion and he quickly replied. "I can't replace a real cop."

"You're going to have to or I'll be a sitting duck. I'll get you a gun and some cuffs. If there are any arrests to be made you can help."

"You're joshing me."

"No. You come ride with me. I might need your help. It's not that hard and I haven't been shot at in over a week. Tomorrow's Saturday so you can sleep as late as you want."

The possibilities and curiosity of such an offer had Colton fully engaged in the conversation. "Really, you want me to come with you?"

"Yes, I do. Put on your running shoes and grab a jacket. We have to be on duty in thirty minutes.

On the way to the station, Daniel outlined what Colton needed to know. "Wait in the car until the shift briefing is over, then we'll get in the cruiser. Whatever happens on patrol, keep your head down and stay in the car. If I need you, I'll holler."

Colton listened intently. Few things capture the

imagination of a twelve-year-old like pulling into a precinct station and seeing twenty patrol cars lined up in a row. After the briefing, Colton saw Daniel exit the building with Garrison. They pulled their patrol car next to Colton.

"Get in the back seat," Daniel told him, "and fasten your safety belt."

The boy was in the patrol car. The shift has just begun. Daniel made no mention of Garrison's presence, and Colton was way beyond any of that. He listened intently to the conversations on the radio. The bright lights from the police car console focused his attention, and Colton leaned forward to see better.

Garrison was in on the plan. Having a minor in an on-duty patrol car was stretching acceptable procedure to the breaking point. In the normal course of activities, ride alongs had to be adults who had gone through basic instruction on police policies and procedures, But Daniel could come up with no other options to reach the boy. If a night on police patrol didn't shake the kid from his doldrums, Daniel didn't know what would. He would take the chance the shift would be safe. Daniel prayed he didn't get the boy hurt with his experiment.

They answered one call of too many men loitering at the corner of a convenience store. Such gatherings were usually drug dealers peddling their wares. Daniel and Garrison disbursed them with the promise they'd be arrested if they returned. The next hour or so was uneventful until, while they were waiting at a stoplight, a car flew past them. Daniel hit the lights and siren and the chase was on.

The car fled south on Northwest Highway. The white Acura reached speeds of 90 mph. The car would soon cross I-30 east of town. If it got on the freeway, speeds could easily exceed 100. Colton braced his arms against the seat and the door. Scenery flew by. Colton held his breath. Thumps in the road sounded like a bass drum inside the car. Minor bumps lifted him out of his seat.

Daniel remained on their tail. The Acura continued south past the interstate. It hit three green lights in a row. As it approached another intersection the light just turned red. The escaping vehicle flew right through the light without slowing down one bit. Colton gripped the seat between the two men and pulled himself forward and watched in breathtaking excitement as the cruiser pursued. Then it happened. The Acura hit something in the road or slightly overcorrected and the vehicle jerked left. The minor error was cataclysmic. The Acura hit a light pole and became airborne. It flipped twice in the air, landed on its side, and rocked over on its top.

Daniel screeched to a stop on the inside lane. Billows of steam erupted from the Acura's cracked engine. There appeared to be a trapped passenger in the car, but the driver managed to exit and ran into the darkness on the other side of the street. Daniel sprinted after the driver. Garrison called fire and rescue.

Daniel had the man in sight. The man ducked between houses, headed for an open field when Daniel leveled him with a crushing tackle. The two crashed to the ground and rolled. Daniel had a knee in the man's back before he could groan twice, and the cuffs went on before he could struggle. When the two appeared under the streetlights, Colton's expression beamed with amazement.

Daniel pushed the man against the squad car and opened the door. "Get in the front seat and stay down. If this pathetic excuse for humanity starts blabbing, let me know." Colton's gaze was glued on the man. He was a grimy looking creep, dirty, sweaty, and catching his breath. The guy didn't look interested in whining or swearing. He had other problems to consider.

The car was stolen. The fire department took charge of freeing the trapped passenger. Daniel and Garrison had a suspect to book downtown. Garrison drove while Colton sat in Daniel's lap. "We're going to have to take you back to the house before we go downtown," Daniel said. "I know that wasn't much to see, but police work is pretty boring."

Garrison threw Daniel a knowing glance.

When they reached the house, Colton stepped out and turned to Daniel. "That was really cool. Thanks, dad."

CHAPTER TWENTY-FOUR

As the years passed, Daniel became entrenched in family life. Colton took to basketball. He grew slender, slowly but surely packing on weight. There was the possibility he'd be taller than his biological father. Melissa and Morgan took dance lessons and became ballerinas. Daniel attended all of their games and recitals.

But Daniel King had a problem not even he understood. His heart was not whole. The vacant space in his soul was not filled by the love of his family. A memory haunted him that would not fade. His attacks on strange men accomplished nothing because there was nothing, in spite of his verbal warnings, that connected his thrashings with what the men had previously done.

Abusive men don't plan their outbursts. Their despicable behavior isn't conspiratorial or orchestrated. Their tirades are impulsive. Their tantrums are incited by the most trivial things. Their depravity is so intense, their brain cells so few that even the fear of death would not dissuade many of them from their domestic violence. Most likely, they have seen abusive behavior toward their mothers or sisters. They foster the infantile belief that women need to be kept in their place and commit acts on female members of their own family they wouldn't do to a neighbor in a million years. If Daniel really thought he was changing the behavior of abusive men, then he was batting zero.

Daniel's unrequited love for Margie was a festering sore that would not heal. It drove him to commit clandestine acts of violence that could not continue. He would be caught or beaten himself. If ever he was forced to account for his acts, he would lose everything, his job, his children, and possibly the only one who had stood by him without question. To be caught betraying Brenda's trust would drive him deeper into despair, into a state of depression he had not yet visited.

Clint's phone calls came less often, but never ceased. On his last call he rattled on about a shopping center being built. He was a part of the ownership group. It was being built on new land in a growing neighborhood. Once finished, it could accommodate twelve to sixteen tenants, depending upon how they parceled the space. He was ecstatic about being part of the action. A steady flow of rental income. "Beats the hell out of one-time commissions on residential properties," he said.

Clint went on about Derek Masters, their quarterback. He and his wife had welcomed twin boys. Denice Brown, a girl he'd dated before Sara, was in China teaching English.

Daniel realized how many people he'd lost contact with from college, and high school, too. Even the people he felt close to slipped away–careers, marriages, circumstances pulled them into other spheres before anyone realized it. Even those whose addresses he had, he never wrote. Maybe a Christmas card to sign and send. Let Hallmark write the greeting. Then there were birthdays. Would he write anything to go along with 'Happy Birthday?' Usually not.

Clint called again six months later. The ten-year anniversary of their university graduation. Was he going to the homecoming football game?

Daniel rubbed his face and sat back in his chair. Clint's phone calls always lasted a while. But homecoming? The word brought back chilling memories. Atherton was less than 200 miles away, and the date was two months off. Daniel hadn't even considered going back to watch a game.

"Are you driving all the way from Memphis for a game?"

"Ten years, my friend. If you want to see some familiar faces, this would be the time to go. Besides, Sullivan, Faulkner, and Rogers are going. We're all going to ride out together from Dallas. There's plenty of room. Roger's got an SUV the size of a bus."

"Well, sounds like you've got it all scheduled again. Guess I could use a change of scenery. I'll think about it."

"Oh hell, King. There's nothing to think about. We'll be back Sunday afternoon. Come with us. You can pay for my share of the gas."

"Okay, okay, I'll go.

Daniel made arrangements to be off work that weekend. He explained his plan to Brenda. He and some college buddies would attend the homecoming game, watch a parade and attend a dinner. Brenda would have gladly gone along. She was equally pleased to stay at home. Melisssa was only five, Morgan eleven. Colton had hit his teens. The children would be more than a handful on a road trip. Brenda consented with a nod and let Daniel give her a kiss on the cheek.

The crammed SUV ride to Atherton consisted of five large men carrying on as if they were back in college. Sullivan had a cog stuck in his brain singing 'Venus, I'm Your Fire,' and when they all tired of that it was a screeching rendition of 'Bad Moon a Rising.' As much as Daniel enjoyed the camaraderie, he was thankful when they arrived in Atherton. His head reverberated with songs he'd never forget and he needed to stretch.

Saturday morning dawned a perfect day for a parade. Daniel stood on a street corner for an hour and watched a string of vehicles adorned with the school colors of blue and white pass by.

The game was between two strong teams. Atherton University sported six wins against one loss and their opponent, San Angelo State was 5-2. When the men found their seats, the rah-rah college mentality continued as Daniel's four friends spied old classmates. The game was of secondary importance.

Daniel got interested in the game. By the middle of the second quarter the game was tied 3 - 3. Both teams played tough defense. Moving the ball was difficult, scoring for either team was almost impossible. Daniel enjoyed watching good defensive football.

Empty bleacher seats existed toward the end zone. In order to watch the game better, Daniel moved down several rows, out to the 30-yard line. It was there, as he closely watched each play, a woman stepped down the aisle and Daniel politely stood to let her pass. But instead of moving further down the bleacher, she sat beside him.

"Hello, Daniel," she said.

It was Margie. Though she appeared as a phantom her soft voice had him at ease. The rest of the stadium and the people in it became a blur. He could not have told anyone what she wore, only that it was her. For the moment, all he could do was gaze at her beautiful face.

"How are you?" she asked.

"I'm fine."

"I saw Faulkner and Stocker up above and asked if they'd seen you lately. They pointed you out."

"I'm glad they did."

"What keeps you busy?"

Daniel noticed the fine lines around her eyes. He inhaled her familiar scent. "I'm a police officer. One of Dallas' finest."

"Oh, you went ahead with that." Her tone was both commending and incredulous. "I'm glad you're safe. I always knew you were a brave man."

"How about you?"

"I'm just a housewife. I have to go now. Nice to see you." With that she stood and headed back up the stadium steps.

She had sat beside him for all of two seconds. It couldn't have been much more. He wanted to turn to see where she went, but he didn't. He wasn't sure why. Her husband had to be in the stands or she would have stayed longer. Why did she stop at all? Was it to convince herself she'd made the better choice? The football game was now a distant memory. Her appearance had wrecked his weekend. He wished he had touched her hand and asked her to stay just a little longer. Maybe she wanted to, but knew it best she didn't. She was so fascinating and enchanting. Had he been dreaming? He felt good she had thought of him at all.

CHAPTER TWENTY-FIVE

The Rucker's drove back to Spinler immediately after the game. They had come in the day before. Margie met with a few old college friends. It was homecoming and Margie had to plead with Robert for two weeks to get him to come along. She didn't want to go back to her campus without her husband.

Marie had been fussy. Robert was dour the entire time, an expression of his loss of control. The entire weekend his attitude let her know he had made a concession that was almost impossible to bear.

Margie fed Marie and put her to bed. The child was ready for a long night's rest. Robert took a shower and went straight to bed. Margie sat at the kitchen table and stirred her bowl of minestrone soup. She had seen Daniel. The weekend had been a success. She walked quietly into the bedroom and retrieved her notebook from under her mattress and returned to the kitchen and began to write.

Dear D,

I'm glad you came to Atherton with your friends. I enjoyed the game. How about you? Always nice to see the Wildcats win. I thought you looked very sharp. I bet you look even better in your police uniform. You haven't changed a bit. I wish I could have talked to you longer, but my little girl was with us.

I'm so glad you're safe. Dallas is such a big and dangerous city in some parts of town. Now I'm a bit worried about you, but I know you're smart and wouldn't do anything reckless. I truly hope you're happy.

I am. I have a nice house, a sweet little girl, a good job, and Spinler is a nice little town. Little towns are good because you get to know a lot more people. It's really comforting to have a number of people close by who you can call friends. I don't know if I'd like the idea of big city life anymore. I'm glad to know you're in Dallas. I'm just glad to know where you are. It really was good to see you, D. M

Robert Rucker had the complicated brain of a simple mind. He dreamed of vast exploits, yet never tried anything new. His passion for race cars and newfound love of NASCAR was the extent of his involvement in the heart-pounding sport. He dumped a substantial amount of his personal income in other men's car restorations. He would never see a dime of the cars' increased value though he may get to ride in one.

Robert was an only child. His father was an oil pipe warehouseman and distributor. He received inventory from manufacturers and dispatched trucks to the field. He ran his household the same way. He and his mother were ordered around like truck drivers on a schedule. His father often raised his voice but not his hand.

His verbal outbursts were loud and could happen at any moment. His mother became a shell of a woman who literally wore slippers in the house lest she make too much noise. Robert spent his teenage life in his room. His father never took him to a ball game, a movie, a fair, a rodeo, a track meet or a concert. The only place his father ever took him, when he was younger, was to school.

As a married man with a child, Robert longed for some excitement but was loath to take on anything unusual, challenging, or risky. If he wasn't working or sleeping, he was parked in front of the television. Robert became increasingly frustrated with his own inertia. He began to raise his voice when the least little thing didn't please him. Endearing comments to Margie became fewer and fewer. He couldn't find anything to be happy about though there was peace, security, and love all around him. He would hold Marie for a while, let her pull on his shirt and kiss her head. He was just as happy when he put her down. Robert had become his father.

Margie found herself in a black hole of boredom. She had married a man only to become his waitress and maid. Robert wasn't hostile, just inattentive. He had no outside interests outside of classic cars and auto racing. At least he spared her the details. One year, he decided to attend the race at the Texas Motor Speedway in Fort Worth. She tried to beg off, but she couldn't. If she wanted Robert to open up to new things, she had to participate in what he already enjoyed.

They left Marie with a sitter and attended the race. The activity on the race grounds certainly had a carnival atmosphere, but the race was all she feared. The noise of forty race car engines was beyond belief. Only the start of the race held any tension. As the cars spread out and became a string of ants on the back straightaway, Margie wondered what everyone was so excited about. She tried not to let her lack of interest show. She would have preferred a trip to a museum, a concert, or a play. Robert's favorite driver came in tenth and he acted like he'd suffered a personal defeat, once again sullen and pouty. Margie tried to cheer him up with little success. She was tied to an adult two-year-old and she could do nothing but close her eyes and take in a deep breath.

As the years passed, Daniel continued to hear from Clint on a regular basis–his business triumphs, the new son that had been added to the family, a detailed report on what every man who played on his offensive line was doing. Daniel might mention a police call or two. Something with a bit of excitement. Like the bank robbery that was over before it began. As soon as the robber drew his gun, he was shot dead by the security guard he hadn't seen. The police had little to do but a mop up job, interview witnesses, and call the morgue. Such stories satisfied Clint's need for juicy news.

Daniel had to believe that Clint had a shortlist of who he called with his tidbits of news. To call everyone he knew in college would have been a full time job. Clint told him about Janet Simmons, a name he barely remembered. Clint reminded him she was in the glee club and sang at various events. She had an excellent voice and many thought she'd go on to become a well-known singer. Come to find out, she'd become a bank VP in Amarillo and had been sentenced to five years for embezzlement.

"Where do you get all this?" Daniel had to smile after the story about Janet.

"Sara. She's a social media wizard. It's her hobby to track people down just to see what they're up to–Google searches and vital statistics from all over the country. Me, the kids, and her computer. That's my Sara."

"No wonder you're all full of trivia no one else cares about."

"Yeah, I hear you, but she makes it sound so interesting."

"Well then," Daniel hesitated, "has Sara ever mentioned anything about Laura Becker?"

"Ah," said Clint, "that's a blast from the past." A lengthy pause hung on the line. Finally, Clint spoke. "Can't say as she has. I guess Laura stayed out of trouble and probably married some nobody. I can ask Sara to ask around." Again, a long pause held the line. "But would I be right in thinking you'd like to learn the whereabouts of someone else?" Clint tried to sound conciliatory.

"I know you mean Margie. She married a high school sweetheart and moved to a one-horse town in Central Texas. All her talk about big cities and living the high life were nothing but pipe dreams. You know I saw her at the football game. It's all water under the bridge."

"Have you ever tried to contact her otherwise?"

"She's married, Clint. I don't think that's the right thing to do. Besides, I'm over her now."

"Daniel, ole buddy. You know who you're talking to, right? You should listen to yourself. You're no more over her than the likelihood of the sun rising over the North Pole tomorrow morning."

"Good grief. Next time I need a pep talk I'll be sure and call you first. Forget I ever mentioned her name."

"Daniel, I'm your friend. Don't ruin your health dwelling on ancient memories. You have a family, right?"

"No complaints there. Brenda is a sweetheart and three kids are enough for me."

"Well then, keep the faith, bro. Spend your time and attention with them. Life is short. Love those who love you. I'll talk to you again soon.

Chapter Twenty-Six

Shortly after Colton turned fifteen, Daniel thought it time to see if his school house education about females matched the facts. Daniel didn't want to sit him down for an uncomfortable discussion so he casually brought up the subject while they drove along.

"Got a girlfriend?" Daniel asked.

"Not right now."

"Any girls around you have your eyes on?"

Colton gave Daniel the once over. "Kinda, I guess."

"You're old enough to ask a girl out to a movie, you know. There are probably a lot of girls who would probably like to go to a movie with you."

"Okay, is this some kind of a test?"

"No son. No test. I thought maybe you had a question or two about the girls."

"Nope."

"Got it all figured out, have you?"

"I know about the birds and the bees, dad."

"That's all well and good. Save me the trouble." Daniel smiled in Colton's direction. "But there's a lot of girls out there to choose from. How do you find the right one?"

The question hit home. Colton looked perplexed. "Well–some of them are prettier than the others."

"Can I give you a tip?"

"Sure."

"The right girl, Colton, is the one you like to look at and who has an agreeable personality. If you love her, that's all the better. Those three things matter most because the plumbing is all the same below the neck."

Colton did a double take and giggled. "Oh my gosh. That is so funny."

"You don't have to repeat that, and don't say I said it." Daniel waited until Colton quit laughing. "My point, son, you treat women with respect. A good woman is like your right hand, like your mother. I don't know what I'd do without her."

"I know," Colton said.

Treat a woman with affection and they'll make your life all it can be. But understand, some girls will do things they shouldn't because they want the attention of boys. Do you follow me?"

"Yes."

"Real men don't take advantage of women no matter who they are. If you don't care for some girl, let her down as easily as you can, but don't string her along. You understand what I mean?"

"Yes sir, Be honest with people."

Daniel reached over and patted Colton on the shoulder. "I always knew you were a smart boy."

One afternoon, Daniel found Brenda sitting on the edge of the bed as he emerged from the shower preparing for his night shift. He stepped to the mirror with a towel around him as he ran a comb through his hair.

"Hon, you startled me. What's up?"

"I need to talk to you, dear."

"Sure, what's for supper?"

"Spaghetti and meatballs, but it won't be ready for an hour. Would you like a snack?"

"Certainly."

"How about chocolate milk and some graham crackers?"

"That will be fine." He looked her way and smiled, but saw she had something on her mind. He was fully dressed except for his uniform jacket when he stepped from the bedroom and was more curious than anything as he sat at the table.

Daniel took a bite of cracker and a drink of milk before Brenda reached across the table and took his hand. Her eyes were full of concern, a hint of fear, a tinge of disappointment. As sweetly as she could, she said, "my dearest Daniel. I know there is a hole in your heart for another."

He didn't move. He didn't say a word as tears flowed almost immediately, and he faced her without denial or excuses. Daniel squeezed her hand. He did not question her or care about how she had learned. "I'm sorry, hon. "I'm so sorry."

"Daniel." She reached her other arm across to him. "Is this some other woman you've met in town?" She waited, but he remained in a state of shame and self-pity. She handed him a wad of napkins. "I'm here for you. I'll always be here for you. But are you seeing another woman?"

He looked as helpless as a little boy. She had never seen a grown man cry, and Daniel was consumed with a purging borne of true remorse. Brenda wanted to go to him and hug him and squeeze all the sadness and needless torment from him. But for now she waited.

"No," he sobbed. "I'm not seeing another woman. I would never do that to you. It's a memory of an old girlfriend from college."

Brenda waited for a moment. "Daniel–we all pass by people in life. Some are around for a while. Others we meet on a plane or a bus and never see them again. And for those we know for a time, when they're gone we often don't know why or where they went. You often speak her name in your sleep. You have to let her go."

The revelation and her tender words had him helplessly silent. His eyes grew red and the tears wouldn't stop. Brenda stepped around the table and put her arms around him. "It's alright, Sweetheart. The children and I love you. I'll never let you go. I know what a good man you are.

"I only pray you let this memory fade. It's not healthy and it does you no good." She pulled him around to face her. "Please baby, stop doing anything that perpetuates thoughts of her."

Daniel returned to the bedroom and lay on the bed. Thoughts of Margie didn't tarnish the true affection he felt for Brenda, but he could never do what Brenda asked. He knew Margie was alive and well, and he knew where she lived. He had just seen her less than five months ago at the football game.

PART II

CHAPTER TWENTY-SEVEN

By 2010, Colton had grown into a fine young man, almost twenty-four. He trained to become an HVAC air conditioning tech. The job paid $48,000 a year. His services were in high demand in Texas. Working outdoors, often on rooftops, he took off his shirt. He was as tan as an Hawaiian native and was packing on weight and muscle. He had his own apartment.

Colton rarely entered conversations. He didn't offer opinions. When he did talk his speech was slow and measured. Daniel assumed it stemmed from Colton's childhood, a defense mechanism, a shield against emotional pain.

Colton came to the house one Saturday morning. He hugged Morgan before he sat at the kitchen table. She still lived at the house and was in her final year at the University of Dallas. Melissa had already left to run around with friends.

Colton's visit was casual. Brenda poured him a glass of orange juice. He planned to pick up his girlfriend later and drive to Arlington. They intended to take in an afternoon game of Rangers baseball. The Red Sox were in town.

Daniel came from the bedroom still wearing his police uniform from his night shift. He placed his hand on Colton's shoulder as the young man sat in his chair, then Daniel made a beeline to the coffee pot.

"How's work?" Daniel asked.

"Busy, as usual. I like it that way."

"Would you like some breakfast?" Brenda was at his side still holding the orange juice pitcher.

"Haven't you already eaten?"

"Melissa and I did. She was in such a hurry to go. Can't waste a Saturday in bed when you can waste it at the mall." Brenda's eyes were full of laughter. "But I was about to fix something for your dad and Morgan. I'll fix a plate for you too."

"Thanks, mom."

As they ate, Daniel looked closely at his two, nearly grown, adopted children. He couldn't have been more pleased. Just the fact that Colton had taken the reins to his own education, impressed Daniel. Colton had a good job. He was making good money. Morgan, without exaggeration, was a beacon of beauty among young women. How Heath and Donna Diebold passed on such genes was a mystery never to be solved. But beautiful, Morgan was. And her different expressions made her all the more glamorous. When she was somber and unanimated, her mouth closed and her gaze focused somewhere in the distance, her smoky, alluring beauty was undeniable. When she smiled, her eyes lit up of course, but her entire countenance came alive. Morgan's infectious smile uplifted everyone who saw it.

Then Daniel said to Colton, "I need to talk to you before you go."

"What is it?"

"It's private," Morgan said. "Dad wants you to help him solve a crime and it's strictly on a 'need to know' basis." Her enchanting expression lit the room and Brenda beamed too.

"Okay." Colton took a final drink of orange juice and followed Daniel to the bedroom where he sat in a corner chair and Daniel sat on the edge of the bed.

Daniel put his arms on his thighs and leaned toward Colton. "Your father has been granted parole and released from prison."

Colton's expression didn't change and he remained quiet.

"I thought you'd want to know. I thought you should know," Daniel said. "He'll be at a halfway house for a while, but he may try to contact you. If you don't want to see him, tell him so. If you do, well, that's your business."

When Daniel finished talking, Colton shrugged his shoulders as if the information meant nothing. He stood and headed for the door.

"Have a good time at the game," Daniel said. "I'm glad you stopped by. Give your mom a kiss before you go."

Colton nodded and walked out.

CHAPTER TWENTY-EIGHT

To replay soothing memories of his Margie, Daniel gazed at old photographs of her, then dropped a few in the mail. He knew it was an exercise in foolishness. The pictures were all of Margie–at Six Flags, the Alamo, standing beside a tree in front of the duplex. If she got them, if she saw them, she would know who sent them.

For a moment, at least, she would remember their time together. The adage was so true–'A picture is worth a thousand words.' But what had she thought of them? Did she care in the least? Would even one of them bring a smile to her lips or a moment of reflection? Daniel thought he knew the answer and he wished he hadn't wasted the stamps. Daniel looked at the phone number he had written on the back of a business card. He dialed the number on a cellphone he had set up under another name. Would she even answer or let it go to voicemail?

"Hello."

It was Margie. Just one little word and he knew it was her.

"Hello. Who is this?"

"It's Daniel." An emotional fear gripped him. It almost made him weak. The hollowness, the adrenaline pumping apprehension.

"How are you, Daniel?" Her words were soft and slow.

"I'm fine. I'm still around." A pause hung on the line. "How are you?"

"Oh, we're doing fine, Daniel. I can't complain."

"I'm really glad to hear that, Margie. You always deserve the best."

"And you?"

"I'm married, fifteen years. We have three children, two adopted."

"Daniel, that's so sweet."

Hearing those words crushed his heart. He choked up and mumbled, "I think I better go," and he hung up.

Margie looked at her dead phone, bewildered, vaguely pleased. Daniel had called. She tried to make sense of his contact from out of nowhere. Had he achieved a milestone or had tragedy paid a visit? Whatever, she would listen. A hundred pleasant memories came rushing back from their time together. But something she said had cut him off. She hoped he would call again.

What had it been, nineteen, twenty years? The passage of time, the enemy of all. If she had it to do over—

She thought Robert would take her into the adult world. He had been so smooth. In high school, Robert made her feel like the grandest girl in the female class. He talked to her like her father, articulate, insightful, informed. There were other boys she wanted to talk to, but she now realized they were too shy or confused or downright nervous to strike up a conversation with the opposite sex. Why do girls wait like that? It was, and remains, a dumb taboo of social priorities. If a girl wanted to meet a new boy, she should go up to him and introduce herself.

In high school, Robert had pledged his undying love. Then he up and joined the Marines for a four-year hitch. He was probably frantic when he thought of her. Had she found someone else? Had she moved across the country? When he got discharged and located her in Atherton, he proposed marriage on their second evening together.

Margie was ready to enter the adult world. She accepted Robert's ring and his vow. A woman has to think of her future and with Robert, she was ready to step into it. She told Daniel of her decision and, that night, cried herself to sleep. For months after that, thoughts of Daniel didn't resurface. The move to Fredericksburg and her whirlwind marriage left thoughts of Daniel tucked away. It wasn't until she began writing in the notebook that thoughts of Daniel returned. The more she wrote, the more she thought of him. Letters she wrote in the notebook gave her pleasant recollections of that big, sweet boy from college.

Sadly enough, the most painful goodbyes,

are the ones,

that are never explained.

Jonathan Harnisch

CHAPTER TWENTY-NINE

There were days when Daniel couldn't get to sleep. Brenda bought over-the-counter medicine to calm him and help him rest. And rest, he would. But his deep-seated stress could be relieved in only one way. It was time to confront another domestic abuser.

Tracking dirtbags wasn't all that time consuming. They lived in plain sight. Many of them had been in jail before. What's another night or two in the slammer and a fine for slapping the old lady around? It wouldn't have happened if she hadn't deserved it.

Daniel liked to catch them alone, but he knew the guy named Bruce Keck had a houseful of kids. His woman had slunk back into the house and Bruce was again king of his squalid realm. But Bruce was seldom home. After work, The Cherry Pit was his place of residence.

The bar was a nondescript, one-story building on a side street. A few motorbikes were in the dirt lot, but most were pick-ups of the 1990's vintage. Daniel wore blue jeans and a ski jacket covered with a few patches of ski slopes he'd visited. When he walked in the building, he stood out like a prep boy at a Hells Angels conclave. There were a few women there too, pasty faced and inebriated.

Daniel felt the stares. The whole place sized him up. He bought a can of beer and dropped fifty cents in a pinball machine.

He had no idea if Keck was there and would have found it difficult to recognize him in the dim light. Someone had Conway Twitty on the jukebox moaning away, "It's Only Make Believe." Daniel knew he was out of his element. No one in the place would talk to him, of that he was sure, certainly not about one of their own. He wanted to play another game, but found he was out of quarters. He stepped back and stood against the wall to finish his beer.

A man picked up his beer and moved down the line. He stopped at the corner of the bar and took a final swing of his beer.

"How are you doing, stranger?" he asked as he approached Daniel. His voice sounded even, but a smirk curled his lips.

"Doing fine. Thanks for asking."

"You kinda new around here."

"Oh, I live nearby, but new here, I guess you could say."

"That's what I did say. You just come in here out of the blue?"

"Pretty much. Thirsty. The sign outside says

Bar-Open." Daniel let a patronizing tone ooze from his words. He was pretty sure he was talking to Keck. Daniel recognized him from a photo. His head was as shiny as a cue ball on top, but the hair on the sides had grown over his ears.

"Well, Mr. Thirsty, we kinda have our own little association here. You're not a member. You'll need to leave."

"I'm glad you brought that up," Daniel said. "I'm here to make an application."

The remark brought on an icy stare. "You trying to be funny, Mr. Thirsty?"

Daniel grabbed a napkin and scribbled on it. "Here it is. Short so you won't have too much to read."

Keck moved around the bar and poked Daniel in the chest. He was half a head shorter than Daniel. His bravado came from his dimwit friends who were listening in. They were all paying attention now. Daniel heard a few chairs grate across the cement floor. "Listen, shit head, you're playing games with the wrong person. Maybe you can get mouthy at your parties, but I'm about to gut you."

Without another word, Daniel snatched Keck's head by the back of his neck and slammed his face into the pinball machine. Keck's face erupted in a flow of blood as his face became a pin cushion of shattered glass. He screamed and Daniel kneed him in the groin. Instantly, at least four men stood in front of him, one with a knife. Daniel pulled a short barreled 9 mm from a strap on his ankle.

"Back up, slime balls. Which one of you wants to go to the morgue?"

Daniel backed around the bar. He knew there was a back door. Could he get to it? Would it be locked? All the chains and leather did nothing for the courage of the men who faced him. They all backed away at the sight of the gun. But Daniel forgot to watch the bartender as he made his retreat. The bartender had stepped into an unlit corner and swung a club as he went by. The swing caught him square in the back below the shoulder blades. It felt like it had cracked his spine. Pain shot out his limbs and he fell. He fired a shot in the air, regained his feet, and broke down the door with his bulk as he fled out the back.

He was hurt, but he could move. Daniel feared a broken rib. He ran down an alley, then slowed his pace as he worked his way between two buildings to the street where his car was parked. Had anyone followed him? He knew they wouldn't call the police. The low lifes in the bar were the type who settled scores on their own. Had they seen what way he went? If one or two were on his tail, he'd take care of them. If the entire bar cornered him, he'd have a problem. If he could make it to his car and slip out of the neighborhood he might be okay. He didn't want his license plate taken down. Daniel pulled away from the curb and slowly moved down the street. At least there was no reason to return to this neighborhood. He could scratch Bruce Keck off his list.

When he got home it was 5:15. He called in sick for work, then told Brenda to make some ice packs and put them on his back.

"I'll be alright, hon. I just need some rest. Pulled a muscle. Get me some of those sleeping pills, will you please. I just need to rest."

Brenda did what he asked without question. When she put the ice packs in place, she wiped her hand across his brow to sweep hair from his eyes. "I'll always take care of you, Daniel. I'll always be here. I love you." And she bent over and kissed his cheek.

Daniel had sustained a severe bruise and he felt it for a month. He received a pain medication prescription from his doctor. He worked without complaining, but grimaced every time he exited the squad car. It was obvious to his partner, Garrison, that Daniel was seriously hurt. After two days of watching Daniel barely able to move, Garrison confronted Daniel as they sat in a semi-hidden location and observed the passing traffic.

"I've seen old women move faster than you. What happened?"

"Fell off a ladder, like I said. Thankfully I landed in the yard and didn't crack my head.

"I think you need to request some sick time," Garrison said. "I mean, you're my partner. I depend on you. I'm getting nervous seeing you like this. Have you seen a doctor?"

"Yeah, they X-rayed it. Nothing broken."

"Okay then, what you need is bed rest, cold packs, heating pad, whatever. Really, talk to Sarge and request some time off."

Daniel shook his head and sighed. "Have you seen the paperwork, the questions? And I've heard, the desk calls you constantly to find out when you're able to return." Daniel took a deep breath. "I'd rather stick it out. I'll be as good as new in a week."

Garrison's expression became stern and he turned to face Daniel. "Look here, King. I like you as a person and I like you as my partner. But I'm not jeopardizing my safety because you can't properly do your job." Garrison let his words soak in. "If you don't ask for sick time, I'll do it for you. Make up your mind, but either way you're going to take some time off."

Daniel took sick leave and didn't return to work for twenty days.

CHAPTER THIRTY

Heath Diebold was a free man–as free as twice a month reporting to his parole officer for the next ten years would allow. He had served a little over half of his original sentence. If he managed to stay out of trouble, he might not have to serve the rest of it. The halfway house had gotten him a job at a warehouse off Walnut Hill. He got a place to stay at an old motel turned into rental units near Harry Hines Blvd. The bus ran within two blocks of his job, but it was within walking distance too. It was illegal for him to possess a firearm or enter an establishment that sold liquor. Other than that, Heath was free to live his life. Within a month on the job, he decided to get in touch with his kids.

While Heath was in prison, Morgan wrote to him every few months as she got older, but she never put a return address on her letters. She knew he wasn't a good person but he was her birth father. Much of the trauma she experienced had been filtered through Colton. Colton protected her. He had sheltered her from much of their father's violence.

In one letter, she mentioned that Colton had gotten into the air conditioning business. Heath began his search by calling every HVAC company in Dallas. No one had heard of Colton Diebold. But one lady mentioned a Colton Maxey and another said a Colton King worked for them. Heath made friends with a chain-smoking derelict with an old Chevy truck. The truck ran fine once it was started, and within another month of staking out employee parking lots, Heath located Colton.

One late afternoon, a young man walked directly toward him as he and his friend Joe sat in the truck. The kid was taller, of course, but Heath knew immediately that he was his boy. Heath jumped from the truck and caught the kid as he walked by.

"Hey fella, got a minute?"

Colton turned, stopped, and the blood drained from his face. He faced a nightmare in human form. His eyes zoomed in with a laser stare. "What the hell do you want?"

"Hey boy, I'm out. I've paid for my bad behavior. I want to see you and your sister, that's all."

Colton was slightly taller than his old man, but he hadn't completely filled out. There was plenty of room to pack muscle on his frame. But he would physically take on the ex-con if he had to, real dad or not. Colton was quick and in shape. Heath would be lucky to run fifty yards without collapsing.

"Here I am, old timer. You can see me right now.

As for my sister, she doesn't entertain scum like you."

"Wait a minute now, I'm still your dad so don't be talking to me that way."

Colton shook his head. He was totally disgusted and spoke to Heath like he was nothing more than a bothersome pest. "You have no say with me."

"Is that right? You think your name's King?" Heath choked out a fake laugh. "You're a Diebold, boy. You ain't no different than the last day I saw you."

Colton turned and faced his biological father. He cocked his head, bit his lip, and stared at him with the same defensive, threatening posture he had as a kid. His words were unmistakable. "You lost us when you went to Huntsville. Morgan is of age now, and neither of us can help you. Don't come around again or I'll call your parole officer. I'm sure you have one." With that, Colton got in his truck and drove away.

Heath wrote down the tag number. He'd find out where Colton lived and he'd find his daughter. Morgan would want to see him, and he wanted to see how she looked all growed up.

Twenty-five year veteran detective, Mike Sanders, opened a file on his desk and looked through the latest complaints that had come in with the same MO as the others. Sanders had reviewed the file before. Currently, it held fifty-one complaints. For close to ten years the file had grown. Sanders surmised there were other victims who hadn't filed complaints. But the file had languished over the years. Other cases held higher priorities. Besides, several of the complainants were now serving long prison terms. Three others, Sanders knew, were dead. One had been shot in the face by his wife with a 12-gauge.

Someone out there was gaining access to residences, subduing the man of the house, dishing out a whipping with some threat that he'd be back if the person ever laid another finger on their wives. All of the complainants had histories of domestic violence, some with arrests and convictions as long as your arm. The perpetrator was certainly going after guilty men. But who would go to such lengths? No one had been killed. What especially caught Sanders' eye was the fact that nearly all of the complainants had been tased. Anyone could buy a taser online for around four hundred bucks, but why would anyone do that if there was no profit in the assault. No one had been robbed. The description of the assailant were all extremely similar, a white man, clean shaven, at least six foot.

Likely the perpetrator had experienced domestic violence or seen it dealt out to a woman he cared about. Anyone could be righteously offended by physical violence to females. But how did this person know who was guilty of such crimes? Sanders searched his brain for who might be able to learn who to target. Someone in the court system? Someone in the probation system? Someone in the police or sheriff's department. Sanders knew he could narrow down a list of suspects if he got a single break. This had been going on long enough, and these men didn't deserve the kind of punishment he saw in pictures. Sanders returned the file to the cabinet, but the case was front and center in his mind.

On one routine night of police patrol, Daniel and Garrison pulled up to a run-down apartment complex on South Jupiter Road. Weekly rentals were available, Hourly stays were more common. Prostitutes were on every corner in the area. A fight had broken out between a pimp and a john. The girl was bleeding and had collapsed on the stairs to the second floor. The john was a big fellow and young enough to throw his weight around. The pimp got the worst of it.

Daniel broke up the fight and cuffed them both.

"She stole my wallet, that bitch. Take her in, too."

"Relax, big boy," Garrison said. "We'll take it from here."

Daniel had the pimp on the ground and cuffed. He looked like he could take care of himself. He'd just met the wrong opponent. There were dark circles around his eyes and sores on his chin, signs of a man who spent his life conning other people and doing too much meth. Daniel pulled him to his feet.

"What's your name?" Daniel said.

The man didn't say a word, but as the two faced each other, his eyes widened and the crack of a smile broke through his bloody lip. He took a close look at the name on Daniel's badge. Daniel patted him down and retrieved his wallet. His driver's license read Benjamin Halstead.

"Well, Benny, looks like you bit off more than you could chew tonight, " Daniel said. "What's your girl's name?" The man remained silent.

Garrison put the john in their patrol car and went into the motel unit to search for the missing wallet and other evidence. Daniel waited until another cruiser arrived and placed Mr. Halstead in the back seat. All the while Benny gave Daniel the once over. Daniel turned his attention to the girl. She couldn't have been over seventeen or eighteen. She would be taken to the hospital for her injuries, then transferred to the justice center. And all the while, the smile on the face of Benny Halstead grew larger and larger.

In his forty-four years of life, Heath Diebold managed to lose his job, his wife and his family, and spend fifteen years in prison for making poor decisions. His course of action after he located Colton, seemed to indicate he was determined to make some more. A few days later, Heath slipped into the employee parking lot and let the air out of a tire on Colton's pickup. When Colton came out after a day's work, Heath was there to meet him. Joe remained in his rusty Chevy working on his third pack of smokes.

"I got a spare for you, but I got to talk to you, boy."

"I don't have time for this crap, old man. I should turn you in right now. I bet I could get you a one-way ticket back to Huntsville where you belong."

"Don't say that, boy. I just want to talk."

Colton looked over the flat tire. A look bordering on absolute hate overtook his expression, but he remained in control of himself. "Okay talk, but you're changing the flat."

Heath got to work changing the flat. "What are you doing?" he asked.

"What do you mean? I finished high school, went to trade school, and I have a job. That's how most people do it."

"Yeah, I know,' Heath said, with a hint of true remorse. "I got off on the wrong track. But I will make it better. I'm going to make it up to you and your sister."

Colton's expression had descended into pure contempt. "You killed my mother, you ass hole. There will be no reunion."

"Jeez, boy. I thought you'd at least give me the time of day."

"What the hell do you want me to say? Just looking at you makes me sick. Can't you understand when you're not wanted?"

"I've been out of commission for a while, kid. Give your old man a break, will ya? I need a better job, and I got no contacts."

"What did you do before?"

"Drove a truck, but that won't due now. I can't travel," Heath said.

"No other skills?" Colton shrugged his shoulders in exasperation. "Go talk to an employment agency."

Heath rubbed his week's worth of whiskers. "Could you spare me a few bucks for a week? I hate to ask, but I know I'm going to be short before the end of the month."

Colton looked upon his biological father with the

same disgust he would view a strung out drug addict snoring on the curb. "I'm sorry, I can't help you there." Colton began to look upon the man, not just as contemptible, but as a lingering pest. He would not let the man into his life. If he had to knock his teeth out or report him to authorities, one way or the other, he would be rid of him.

"Let me take your tire," Heath said. "I'll get it aired back up."

"I thought you said you needed money. Think you're going to take this brand new Michelin and sell it. Think again, old man. I'll air up the tire and put it back on, Colton said. "Tell me where you're staying and I'll bring you the spare."

"The old Skylight Motel on Harry Hines at Royal. It's behind a flea market, #6. Maybe a buck or two. Joe needs some gas." Heath pointed at Joe waiting in the truck.

Colton thought about it– "Have you been to my mother's grave?"

"What? Well no, not yet. Ain't been out that long, boy. Been plenty busy."

Colton shook his head, the most contemptible expression settled on his face. "You know, she was your wife." Colton shook his head again as a dumbfounded expression from the other man looked back at him. "You go to her grave and tell me what the area looks like and I'll give you $20. There's something very prominent close to her grave."

"Hey but, how about now?" Heath whined.

"Eternal Rest Gardens," Colton said, "and I'll bring the spare to you tomorrow." He doubted if his father would wise up, but if he came around his workplace again, he would call the authorities. He'd fix his tire, put it back on his truck, and return the spare. Beyond that, he was done talking to his father.

Two months after he first phoned Margie, it was late October, Daniel had the overwhelming urge to try it again. Would she talk to him at all after he'd hung up on her? That was impolite and childish. He could only imagine what she thought of him now. That conversation could have turned into something. She was on the line, she was talking to him. He might have been able to open her up and find out what was going on in her life.

Daniel had no illusions about ever holding her again. Another kiss was beyond the realm of possibility. But if phone conversations were the best he could get, he would take them. He would never hang up on her again. He must hold his emotions in check, because hearing her voice was an answered prayer. He could wallow in euphoric daydreams after they got off the line.

Over time, Daniel pilfered cell phones from arrestees. Many suspects were caught with two or three phones on them, and they certainly didn't own them all. For a month or two the phone would be good until the next bill wasn't paid and the account closed. Daniel used one such phone to call Margie's number again. After the third ring, Margie answered.

"Hello Margie. It's Daniel."

"Hello, Daniel. I thought it might be you."

"I didn't want your husband to see my name in case he answered."

"We each have a phone and we don't eavesdrop on each other's calls." she said. "He's gone now, anyway."

"I'm glad you answered, really glad. I enjoy hearing your voice. I'm sorry I hung up when I called before."

"Daniel, Daniel. I can talk to you, but does it really help anything?"

"What does it hurt? We're just talking. You have to know I have a place in my heart where your memory is stuck forever. There are days when I think about you all the time."

"Oh Daniel, you're so sentimental. Life isn't always what we'd hoped for."

"I'm a cop like I told you at the game. I've seen plenty of life's ugliness."

"Yes, I'm sure you have," Margie said. "And you're a family man?"

"Three kids, like I told you before. I love them all to death. How about you? I heard you had a daughter."

"Yes, one daughter. She's in high school now."

"I bet she's as beautiful as you."

Margie let out her soft, innocent laugh. "I'm almost forty. My daughter is much prettier. You're living in a time that has come and gone."

"I'm okay with that. My memory holds a picture that will never fade."

The line went silent for a lengthy period.

"I think I better go now," Margie said.

"No, stay on the line, please. Tell me what you do?"

"For what purpose, Daniel? I know you're working yourself up into an emotional wreck."

"Not at all," he said. "I know my life is here. If I remember a lovely girl and I want to know she's alive, healthy, and happy–is that a crime?"

"No." The line went silent again and Daniel had the distinct feeling his comments had hit a nerve, but he didn't come right out and ask.

Daniel spoke up to fill the dead air. "My little girl, Melissa, is in high school too. She's in the band. She plays the clarinet."

"What keeps you busy, Daniel?"

"Being a police officer. You were right, Margie. One minute the job is totally boring, the next minute utter chaos. Luckily I've never been shot or shot at anyone else."

"You're a brave man, Daniel. I'm glad you've stayed safe. I guess I knew you wouldn't settle for something routine and predictable."

"How about you, Margie?"

"I have to go, Daniel. I don't want to go down those old roads anymore. No good can come from us rehashing the past. Don't call me again, Daniel. Please just let the past stay in Atherton and from now on . . . " Her voice grew frantic and Daniel cut her off.

"Tell me one thing, Margie. After all these years–just one thing. Why?

She didn't answer him. "From now on, if I see any strange names calling, I won't answer. I'm going to hang up, and I mean it. Don't call me anymore."

"That's all you can say. You ripped my heart out and you can't tell me why?"

"Oh Daniel," She choked back a sob. "I don't know why." And with that, the line went dead.

Daniel looked at an empty screen and felt another pang of separation. He could not have known, Margie had put down her phone, and she fell across her bed and cried into her pillow.

I still belonged to you,

long after you belonged to someone else.

Jenim Dibie

CHAPTER THIRTY-TWO

The next day Benny Halstead posted bond. A night in jail was the cost of doing business. He had to keep his girls working. At times he had to protect them too. He had been booked on minor charges. His lawyer would get them dismissed.

But Benny had a nugget of information of much greater interest than his legal problems. His clan would salivate at the news. He couldn't wait to get to the Cherry Pit to spill his guts. His fellow cohorts of leather and chains would buy him drinks. He would be showered with accolades. His sharp eye and quick mind had a police officer on the hot seat and the cop didn't even know it yet.

Benny walked into the Cherry Pit at 10:00 a.m. He hadn't taken more than two steps into the place where Deacon, the bartender, had a bottle of Shiner Bock on the bar.

"Got a free night of accommodations, all expenses paid."

"Oh yeah. How's that?" Deacon asked.

"Lew Sterrett, an excellent facility."

Deacon laughed. "What happened?"

"Crystal got into an argument with a john. I had to step in. Got a busted lip for my trouble. He tried to say Crystal took his wallet but I knew he was lying. Anyway, I figure he's got bigger problems than me. I bet he has a wife, a job. How's he going to explain being thrown into jail?"

Deacon listened but remained quiet as he moved up and down and wiped off the bar.

"But listen. I got something that'll blow your mind."

Deacon kept wiping.

"Remember that guy who busted up Keck's face?"

"Of course. I almost got the guy in the back of the head with my club. Wish I had. He wouldn't be out running free."

Benny leaned across the bar and waited until Deacon stepped closer. "I know who he is."

Deacon finished wiping. "Really? You're not shitting me?"

Benny shook his head with the authority of a man who knew something.

"Who is he?" Deacon was paying attention now..

"He's a cop." Benny let the words hang in the air.

"You sure?"

"No doubt. I know it's him. It's the cop who arrested me last night."

"Wow!" Deacon was truly impressed. "Get a name?"

"Yep–King."

"Keck will love to hear this. Have you seen him lately?" Deacon asked.

"No."

"He came in a week ago. Those cuts have healed, but I swear, the guy's face looks like a potato."

"We can definitely cause the cop to lose his job," Benny said.

"Yeah, but Keck's going to want a whole lot more than that. We have to tell him. He's good at coming up with a plan. Keck will want to make him suffer."

When Bruce Keck got word that the man who had smashed his face into a pinball machine was a cop, a grotesque grin formed on his face and he hugged Benny with an arm across his back.

"Y'all hear that? The cop that busted up my face works the night shift in East Dallas. I say we cause a disturbance, and see if he comes to the scene . If he does, we ambush him and put him in the hospital. We ain't gonna kill nobody, just hurt him bad. Who's with me? Free drinks for those who join in." Keck raised his mug and the bar let out a cheer.

Later that day, Detective Sanders got an anonymous phone call.

"Detective, are you familiar with the incident of a man getting his face smashed into a pinball machine a while back?"

"I'm familiar with it," Sanders said.

"Well ugh, I know who did it."

Sanders sat up in his chair and leaned over his desk. "And who would that be?"

"Is there a reward?"

"There's $1,000 for information that leads to an arrest."

"Okay then, I want my name on record. It's Benny Halstead. I have some friends who want to ambush the guy and teach him a lesson. I'm not in for that. I don't want nobody getting hurt."

"You're on record," Sanders said. "You got a name?"

"Yeah, the guy's one of your own. His name is King."

CHAPTER THIRTY-THREE

After the encounter with his biological father, Colton drove in the direction of his apartment, but then he turned and headed to Daniel and Brenda's. Maybe a mention of this to a real police officer would shed light on what he really could or couldn't do when it came to Heath. The man was a menace to him and Morgan no matter that they were now adults. A restraining order would likely be Daniel's recommendation, but that would involve a court appearance and payment to a lawyer. Maybe Daniel knew an easier, quicker way to make the older man mind his own business.

Brenda was delighted to see him and gave him a big hug. Colton kissed Melissa on the cheek. Morgan was away at the time. Daniel hadn't been up that long and was shaving, preparing for another night of police patrol.

Colton stepped into the bathroom and leaned

against the door frame. 'My old man has found out where I work. Today was the second time he's been there and today he flattened one of my tires so I couldn't drive away."

Daniel turned from the mirror and faced the young man. "He cut your tire?"

"No–he let the air out. He had a spare. He knew it would buy him time to whine and make excuses."

"What did he want?" Daniel asked.

Colton shook his head. "It really doesn't matter, dad. The reason I stopped by is to know how I can get rid of him permanently."

Daniel wiped off his face, splashed on aftershave, and pulled on a T-shirt. "Let's go to the bedroom where we can talk in private." Once in the room, Daniel shut the door and they sat near the window. "Your mother and sister don't know anything about what I'm going to tell you. I want to keep it that way." Daniel paused and took a deep breath. He brought his hands together as if in prayer and rubbed them up and down over his mouth.

"I trust you'll keep to yourself what I'm about to tell you."

Colton's eyes opened wide with curiosity and apprehension.

Daniel reached over and put his hand on Colton's knee. "Don't worry, son. It's nothing strange. It's straightforward." Daniel paused and inhaled a deep breath. "For almost as long as I've been a police officer, I've been seeking out men who beat their women and giving them an ass whipping."

Daniel waited for the statement to sink in. Colton got the gist of it immediately. "I've read about a vigilante of that sort in the paper every once in a while. Has that been you?"

"If I've saved even one woman a kick or slap or having something thrown at her, it's all been worth it. That's the truth and I don't apologize for it one bit. Any problems?"

"Jeez no, dad. That's freaking courageous, I mean, you had to have had some close calls. That's fantastic."

"Enough. I didn't do any of it for money, or praise. I did it for the victims. If you want to send Heath a message, we can work together and make him disappear of his own free will."

"I'm all in. I know where he stays."

The time was almost five p.m. Daniel had to go on duty at eight. They had just enough time to make one Heath Diebold disappear for good. The men each drove their own vehicles to Heath's address. Daniel stopped a half block away. He would walk up, size up the 'lay of the land,' and see what Colton and Heath were doing. With all the years that had passed, Daniel doubted Heath would remember him at all.

The old motel layout was a semicircle of one-story units each with a carport. Colton had pulled up in front of the carport of #6, and unloaded the spare tire and rolled it beside the door.

No one else was outdoors as Daniel walked by as if he was walking through the complex. He heard Heath begging for more money from Colton.

The sound of Heath's voice and the sight of his face immediately jolted Daniel with a shot of adrenaline, and he wanted to beat the man to a pulp. Within feet of him was the man who had traumatized his own children and left them alone and defenseless. For more than ten years, Daniel had taken those kids and nurtured them as though they were his own.

Daniel was always home when they got back from school. He helped them with their homework. He wanted them to know there was a lot more to America than Dallas, Texas, and there was a lot more to the world than the United States. Daniel did his best to help all three of his children with their math and writing assignments. And now, within earshot, was the two-bit, wife beating loser trying to horn into his son's affairs and upset his life. If there ever was a time, he wanted an abuser to pay with pain, it was now. Embarrassment and humiliation coupled with a dose of honest to god fear was not Daniel's idea of just payback for Heath Diebold. He wanted to hurt the man, and hurt him bad.

But as he circled back, and got closer to the two men, Daniel realized he could do no such thing. He couldn't let Colton see violence as a way to solve problems. He had spent too much time and tears on the boy to flush it all in one misguided assault. Now he wished he'd never told Colton of his clandestine activities in spite of the young man's enthusiastic approval. The plan to knock Heath around, read him the riot act, and send him on his way vaporized in Daniel's mind. He would have to get Heath to leave Colton alone in some other way.

Heath's head snapped around when he felt the presence of another person. "Whadda you want?"

Daniel smiled and stood in Heath's space. "I'm here to help you understand what's best for you."

"What's that supposed to mean? Get back, and mind your own business."

Daniel grabbed Heath by the arm and pushed him into the housing unit. Colton followed.

Heath yanked his arm away. "Who in the hell are you? Colton?"

"This is my dad."

Heath's face turned white.

"And we're going to have a little heart to heart talk."

"Piss on you. I don't answer to you." Heath grabbed a cheap plastic ashtray and threw it at Daniel. The ashtray missed Daniel and he pushed Heath into a worn chair with batting poking through numerous holes in the cloth.

"Don't move," Daniel warned him. "Try to get up and I will have to hurt you."

Heath's face screwed down tight and he hyperventilated through his nose. He could have bit a nail in two if he'd had one in his mouth, and he wanted to move, but Daniel stood over him.

"Your life has changed since you went to Huntsville, Heath," Daniel said in a smooth yet commanding tone. "The world has changed and all the people you once knew. You forced that outcome on yourself. You have no one to blame for your circumstances but yourself."

"Yeah, you're full of empty words. Mind your own damn business."

"I am. This young man is my son. Not yours. Let that sink in." Daniel waited a few seconds. "I know the drill with your parole office. Colton and his sister don't have to get a restraining order against you. No, bright boy. You're an ex-con, and if someone doesn't want you around, all they have to do is sign an affidavit. Contact them again after that, and you'll be getting refitted for another orange jumpsuit."

Heath was so enraged he couldn't speak.

"So if you want to return to prison, keep it up. I'm going to keep my eyes on you," Daniel said.

"It's not fair," Heath whined. "I just wanted to see my kids."

Colton stood against the front door and spoke up. "No one believes you. Have you done anything to show you're not still selfish, deceitful, and dishonest? Not to mention, a ticking bomb with your anger and emotions."

"Here's the bottom line, Diebold," Daniel said. "Don't contact Colton or Morgan, period. Don't try to find out where they live. Don't call, don't write." Daniel stuck out his open palm in Heath's face. "See this hand? If I ever see you again, I'll squeeze your nuts into Play Dough. They don't want your apologies or to hear your excuses. Got it?"

Heath just stared at the empty wall in front of him.

"This is your one and only warning. Don't make another bad decision."

With that, Daniel and Colton walked out.

CHAPTER THIRTY-FOUR

Daniel dressed at the precinct and put his civilian clothes in his locker. He prayed for a quiet, uneventful shift. The night was anything but–he and Garrison responded to a shooting at a gas station, a burglary in progress, pulled over a DUI suspect, gave the woman a field sobriety test which she failed, and escorted her to jail.

During the entire shift, Daniel worried if Heath would take the friendly advice. He had handled it the best he knew how. He was glad he hadn't hit him. In spite of his disgust with his birth father, Colton wouldn't have wanted to see that. Daniel had been nervous through the entire encounter. His fervent hope was that Heath would wise up, at least once in his life, and disappear from the lives of Colton and Morgan.

During the long and busy night shift, Daniel's thoughts also turned to his actions against abusers.

It was not only counterproductive, it was wrong. He was only able to carry out such violent attacks because of his size and youth. That didn't give him the right to enforce his own brand of justice. He had excused himself with Colton by saying 'if I saved one woman from being slapped . . .' but had he helped even one woman? He had to stop. He would stop. He was not remorseful or relieved. He was simply finished.

After this evening's encounter with Colton and Heath, Daniel realized his clandestine attacks on other men, no matter the dregs of society they might be, was misguided. Their beatings didn't help him forget Margie. Daniel looked forward to the end of the shift. Finally, he could go home and get a home cooked breakfast and some rest.

But as soon as he walked into the station the duty sergeant called him in. "Going to need a little more of your time, King. A detective wants to see you."

Daniel groaned. If a detective needed information on a case why couldn't they ask questions at the beginning of a shift? He was physically tired and mentally exhausted and ready to go home.

Detective Sanders led Daniel to an interrogation room. "Have a seat officer. I just have a few questions about a case I'm working on." Sanders shuffled some papers while Daniel tried to adjust to a comfortable position in his chair.

Sanders raised his head and looked straight at Daniel. "Officer King, have you heard of the Cherry Pit Lounge?"

The question seemed to come from nowhere and

for a moment it didn't click. "No, can't say as I have." Daniel involuntarily cleared his throat. "No place with that name on my beat."

"Anywhere in town?" Sanders asked.

"I don't go to bars. I'm married. I have a family."

"Well then, do you know a man by the name of Bruce Keck?"

"No, not at all. What's this all about?"

"Officer King, I'd be glad to tell you. Seems like this Keck fellow got his face pulverized a few months back, and someone comes to us and says you did it."

"No, no, detective. I go strictly by the book. If I'd had any dealings with this Keck guy, I'd have written a report on it."

Sanders nodded as though in agreement. "You know what I found interesting about Mr. Keck's past."

"What?"

"He has two convictions on his record for domestic violence. Spent six months at county in '05. Broke his wife's arm and knocked out three of her teeth."

"Sounds like a regular altar boy."

"The reason I mention that, King, is we've been having a spate of vigilante retributions on men who abuse their female partners. They may deserve it, but we have laws in this country. You know anything about that?"

"No, I don't, but I am interested in how I got connected to this Keck fellow."

"Okay listen, Officer King." Sanders' tone went

from cordial to serious, his expression from congenial to stern. "I need you back here at 9 a.m. in civilian clothes. You're going to be part of a lineup."

"What? I know you're not kidding, but c'mon. You don't really think I'm out beating up civilians, do you?"

"You're a big man. I don't know what you might be doing out of uniform. Just be back at nine. Don't make this more difficult than it has to be. Nobody but me and some guys in the precinct are going to know you're a cop. Others have participated in lineups before. Let's do it and get it over with."

Daniel left the station in total panic. He could never go back. Life as he knew it was over. His brain fired scattered shots of confusion through his mind. Someone had mentioned his name. Nothing that could be proven one-on-one. But a lineup. The very thought filled his heart with terror. He had never worn a mask, and they would no doubt have men who filed reports staring at him through the one-way glass. If he were identified, and he would be, they'd have enough to file charges. He was done. His career was over. He could never admit what he'd been doing to Brenda and the girls, and he felt ashamed. If he was about to lose his freedom, there was one thing he must do before he was locked away. He had to go. He had to try.

Chapter Thirty-Five

When Daniel got home, Brenda had breakfast ready as she always did. "I'll be out in a minute, hon. I'm going to change first." Daniel took off his utility belt and locked his sidearm in the safe. He sat on the bed with his head in his hands. He knew he was finished–numerous counts of assault and battery. He felt so sorry for Brenda, how she trusted and believed in him. And the girls. They would never understand how their sharp and upright police dad ended up in prison. He changed into civilian clothes.

He entered the kitchen with a glum expression, but Brenda immediately knew there was a problem. She smiled and put a plate of eggs and bacon in front of him. "What's the matter, dear? Rough night?"

The realization of what confronted him broke through and tears filled his eyes. "I have to go away for a while. Please take care of the girls. In Spinler–

I'll be back, but I don't know when." Brenda grew frightened. Daniel took her and hugged, then extended his arms and gazed into her trusting face. "I'm so sorry, baby." He again pulled her to him and kissed her.

"Daniel, stay. Let me help you." But he turned and walked from the house without touching his breakfast.

Brenda was so shaken, she immediately called Colton at work. "I've never seen him like that before." She began to break down. "Your father is going to do something terrible, Colton. I can feel it. Please please, don't let it happen."

"Where's he at?

"He said something about Spinler, Colton, but I don't even know what that is."

"That's got to be a person or a place. I'll find him, mom. He'll listen to me."

Throughout the three hour trip to Spinler, Daniel conditioned himself to accept his fate. He was a criminal and a fugitive. His future was a darkened corridor, and the door at the end was bolted shut. He would see Margie one last time. She would see him. He knew she would. Their phone conversations had been wonderful. He would subdue her husband, if he was around, and spend time with her–whatever amount of time he had. He would not leave Spinler, Texas, until he held Margie in his arms once again.

It was late morning when he arrived in the town. A bleak testament to small towns all over the Midwest. Main Street was as wide as a football field with hardly a car in sight. There was a five-story abandoned hotel two blocks from the train depot. Daniel saw the congregation of vehicles around the only obvious restaurant in town with the catchy and highly original name The Spinler Diner.

A search for a Motel 6 or a Best Western was fruitless so Daniel took a room under an assumed name at the Cactus Wire Motel. It was not an overstatement to say the place had seen better days–far better days. The mattress springs had been so throttled by lovers they squeaked when he even touched the bed. When he turned down the blanket the sheets looked more dingy than white. The bathroom faucet maintained a steady, metronome drip and an amateur painting of a cowboy and a horse around a campfire hung on the wall. The horse looked more like a camel.

Robert Rucker was the source of all his problems. Intellectually, Daniel knew that wasn't true. But emotionally, once he learned the name, Daniel couldn't shake the words from his brain. And somewhere in this town, he could be found.

Rucker worked at a Ford dealership. He'd be around a lot of people during the day. Maybe he could catch him alone during his lunch hour. Maybe he could catch him at home when Margie was away. First, he had to find out what the guy looked like.

Daniel sat in the motel room a few minutes more. He felt so alone and incompetent. All his work on the police force amounted to a mirage of people, some good some bad, who floated through his life for a moment, only to be gone forever. He thought of Brenda. She was such a good woman, a wonderful mother. He cared for her, thought the world of her, but he knew he didn't love her. He couldn't help it. As much as he tried to compensate, his marriage was a fraud, and he feared Brenda knew it, too.

Daniel approached the receptionist at the dealership.

"Is there a Robert Rucker here?" The question clenched his throat. He was terrified he'd be told, "Yes, he's right over there."

He didn't want to talk to a car salesman.

But without any hesitation, she said, "he's in the parts department," and she pointed the way.

At the parts counter he ordered a 5-quart jug of motor oil. The name tag on the man helping him said BOB. Bob is short for Robert and he wondered. But the guy was too young to be Rucker.

Daniel saw at least four men working in the department and he closely watched them all. Only one could match the man he was looking for. He was inputting information into a computer behind the sales counter, and Daniel's focus zeroed in on him.

The man was slender and definitely older than the rest of the crew. He had a thick, wide mustache that would make Sam Elliot envious. His eyes were dull and his cheeks slightly shrunken. The guy looked like he'd be as much fun as a migraine headache.

Daniel took the motor oil back to his car and tried to come up with his next move. He had a face and an address. He may be able to double check the name in the local directory. There was no phone in his motel room, but the office did have a phone book. He looked up the name Rucker, and there it was–622 Sycamore Lane. Everything matched up. He took a pen and drew a big circle in the book,

A chill of guilt and doubt made him cold. He should never have said anything to Brenda about where he was going. He would never see her again, or precious Melissa, and loveable Morgan. He wanted to go back, but it was too late. He had assaulted dozens of men over the years. The unlawful blows to another person was battery and a felony. An ex-cop can't spend time in prison. He'd be in solitary forever for his own protection. He'd go crazy. He couldn't do it. He had no other options.

If he could get one last hug and kiss from Margie–he inhaled deeply, closed the phone book, and handed the pen back to the clerk. Daniel got back in his car. Sycamore Lane couldn't be that hard to find.

CHAPTER THIRTY-SIX

After listening to Brenda's pleas, Colton knew he had to act. The previous day he prayed his birth father would disappear. He'd been upset about the confrontation between the two men he'd called father at different times in his life. Colton fell asleep, his face wet with tears, his body exhausted.

When he awoke, his entire attitude had changed. He knew in his heart Daniel was a good man. He understood all the good things Daniel and Brenda had done for him and Morgan. He would stake his claim on the future and let go of the past. There were things a person could not change. Some things, he realized, were going to knock you down. But a person had to move on. To wallow in the past was to waste your life.

He called Garrison. They had become friends

over the years. Maybe he knew where his dad was going, maybe he knew what was on his mind.

"My dad's left town," Colton said, "and I think he's headed for trouble."

"We have a shift tonight."

"I don't think he'll be back."

"What did he say?"

"Have you ever heard of Spinler? What is that?" Colton paced as he switched the phone to his other ear.

"Not someone we arrested recently. Pretty sure of that," Garrison said. "Maybe it's a business or a location. Have you looked on a map?"

"I don't have a map."

"Just a second." Garrison went to his computer and pulled up a map of Texas and entered the name. "It's a town, Colton, looks like 200 miles from here."

"I've got to go find him."

"You stay put. I'll call down there and have them look for his car. I've got the plate number. If he's in trouble or danger, they'll handle it. You go stay with your mom. Understand? Colton, do you hear me?" The phone went dead.

Sycamore Lane was a quiet street with large lots. The street was an asphalt road without curbs, a peaceful, shaded area. The house had a wide drive. Both garage doors were closed. He drove by the house and saw the address on the mailbox. But Daniel didn't like the layout. There were few fences.

Neighbors could see anyone trying to break into a house. It was going to be dark soon. He headed back to the motel.

At least he was now in Spinler. He had but one objective. Daniel went to bed early, because he got up at three. He was used to being up at night and he had a good five mile walk ahead of him to Sycamore Lane. He carried plastic gloves, plastic tie-straps, his Taser, and a small crowbar he ran down inside his pant leg and hooked the curved end over his belt. He left the short-nosed pistol hidden in the car. He didn't want to scare Margie or make his legal matters worse. He kept to side streets, away from streetlights as he made his way. When he got to the neighborhood, he walked right down the middle of the road. There were no streetlights except intersections, and he didn't have to pass through one. Once at the Rucker's house he crept along the lot boundary to hopefully escape any motion detectors. He crawled up to the house at a corner with no windows and he sat down with his back on the brick facade and checked his watch.

It wasn't even 6:00. He was here. He would wait. It was Saturday. Whoever was in the house might sleep late. If he saw Margie leave by herself, that would be an excellent break. But even if the two of them spent the whole day together, he would separate and subdue Mr. Robert Rucker before the day was over. Daniel sat on the west side of the house, hidden by bushes, with a clear view of the driveway. He leaned against the house. He could handle a stakeout. He'd had plenty of practice.

CHAPTER THIRTY-SEVEN

Colton left for Spinler the moment he got off the phone with Officer Garrison. He arrived in town at one in the morning. The town was as quiet as a parishioner at communion. Even the convenience store he drove by was closed. He found one motel named Happy Trails Inn. Colton searched the parking lot for his dad's car. It wasn't there.

He found another motel at the far west end of the town called The Cactus Wire. He spied the car immediately. From the way the car was parked, however, he couldn't tell what room Daniel might be in. He rang the outside office bell. After several minutes of ringing and no answer, Colton beat upon the door.

A disheveled woman in a housecoat finally pulled back the curtain and cracked open a sliding glass window. "No vacancy, must go," she said.

"We closed."

Colton grabbed the window and yanked it completely open. "Daniel King. What room is he in?"

The woman's expression registered astonishment and fear. Lingering nocturnal cobwebs instantly evaporated from her brain, and she was fully awake. Colton reached for her but she yelped and pulled away. "I call police."

Colton backed away from the window. He might as well wait for the police. He would tell them his story. At least he had found Daniel. He could stop him from doing anything stupid.

A police car did arrive. Colton raised his hands standing beside his truck and was quickly illuminated by a high-powered spotlight.

"Turn around, put your hands behind your head, and get on your knees," came the command from behind the light. Colton was cuffed and stood in front of the cruiser.

A single officer held a flashlight in his face. "Okay, fella. What's all the commotion about?"

"Okay, Daniel King is a police officer from Dallas. He's here in town and I'm not sure why, but I don't think it's for anything good."

"What's it to you?" asked the cop.

"He's my dad. Did your office get a call from Dallas about him–to be on the lookout for his car?"

"Not that I'm aware of."

"Look officer, I'm just trying to keep anything bad from happening. He's not dangerous. Really, he's not. But a lot of things have happened lately and I'm afraid he's a little unstable."

The officer took the flashlight beam from Colton's face.

"Can you get the clerk to tell you what room he's in? Everything can be resolved, and I'll get him back home. I'm sorry any of this happened."

The officer thought for a moment. "You stand right here. Do not move." He rang the night bell and knocked on the door. When the woman answered, the officer asked about the car. The woman wasn't sure as she didn't have anyone registered named Daniel King. But many of her guests were regulars–workers who came and went. She narrowed it down to room #9.

The woman threw Colton a hateful glance as she walked to the room. The officer walked behind her.

Several knocks at the door brought no response. She used her key and opened the door. The room was empty. Both the woman and the officer looked about. Someone had used the room, but there wasn't anything left. Unless extra clothes and other items were in the car, this person hadn't planned for a long term stay.

"Okay, you can lock it up for now," the officer told the woman, then followed her back to the office. What can you tell me about the guy who rented that room," he asked.

"He very nervous."

"Did he say why he was in town?"

She shook her head, then added. "He very nervous. He write in my book."

"What?"

She pulled the phone directory out from under the desk. "He write in my book."

The officer opened the book and flipped some

pages. There were a number of marks in it, some pages dogeared. The officer wasn't completely sure what she meant.

And then, she made a circle in the air with her finger.

The officer understood completely. "I'll have to take this as evidence, and don't clean out #9. Our office will be in touch with you." He stepped outside and turned to Colton. "For now, you're coming with me."

CHAPTER THIRTY-EIGHT

At a quarter till eight, Daniel saw a pick-up truck leave the house. From what he could see, it appeared to be Rucker behind the wheel. He figured Margie was still there, possibly with her daughter. He was only after Rucker, and Rucker was currently away. He would spend his last moments as a free man with Margie. She may be anxious, momentarily afraid, even angry. But she would be there. He could calm her down. For whatever time he had, she would be near.

There was no reason to wait any longer to gain access into the house. He stood, stretched. He found two small windows away from what was obviously the master bedroom with its huge translucent pane in the bath. Daniel popped off the screen and gently pried the plastic frame up the slides. He poked his head inside the room and found it empty. With a jump, his thighs were over the sill and he pulled himself into the house.

The house was a single level ranch, sparsely furnished, open and light. There were a few affirmations of the Southwest motif, Navajo rugs, a framed drawing of a sun-bleached cow skull. Daniel went straight to the refrigerator and drank half a quart of milk. There were strawberries in a bowl and a half of a tomato. He ate it all. As he pulled his head from the refrigerator, Daniel saw a young woman, a robe wrapped around her, standing in the doorway.

She jumped when she saw the man was not her father. Daniel was caught off guard, as well.

"Oh my god," she cried and tried to run.

Daniel caught her and pulled her up straight by her arms. "I'm not here to hurt you. Just relax." But as he held the young woman's arms, Daniel could not believe what he saw. She was college age Margie all over again. He truly couldn't believe the resemblance. "Are you Marie?" The girl nodded. "Where's your mother?"

And in a matter of seconds, Daniel witnessed a face of fear transform into one of abject despair.

"Who are you?" she asked.

"An old friend."

"You don't know?"

"Know what?"

"Let me go." Daniel did and she stepped back. "My mother is dead."

The words brushed past his ears like a mosquito zooming by and he thought the girl had misspoke. "What did you say?"

The tears and the redness came to her eyes, and when she said it again Daniel could hardly stand."She died last Sunday. The funeral was yesterday."

Daniel couldn't think. He had just talked to her on the phone, and had heard her voice only days ago. Was it last Sunday? Yes, it might have been. Daniel collapsed into a nearby chair. "What happened?"

"The doctor said a heart attack. She died in her sleep." Marie damped her tears and blew her nose, but she was no longer afraid of the giant intruder. "You're Daniel, aren't you?"

He nodded.

"I don't know how many bedtime stories I've heard that included a character named Daniel," she said.

"She was still young. A heart attack? How is that possible?

"Women have heart attacks. That's all the hospital would say."

Daniel plied his scalp with his fingers. When he looked up, his face was creased with sorrow. Daniel was completely lost–mind and spirit, and Marie placed her hand on his shoulder. "We all miss her."

"Will you take me to the cemetery?"

"Yes, but you better open the front door while I change. I called the police–speed dial on my phone. They know the address. I'll tell them it was a mistake."

A 911 call came into the police station. The officer looked at the address–622 Sycamore. He instantly knew the address was on his list of circled addresses from the telephone book. He grabbed the keys to the cell. Colton popped up from the bunk and grabbed the bars. "You can come with me," said the officer. "We just may have the location you're looking for,

A police car rounded a corner as Daniel stepped onto the porch.

"That's him," announced Colton. "That's my dad."

The squad car turned off the strobe lights as it stopped in the drive.

"What's the emergency?" the Spinler officer asked.

Daniel pointed inside. "Young lady is getting her things together. She'll fill you in."

"And you are?"

"Daniel King. I'm a police officer in Dallas." He showed the other officer his badge and credentials.

"Okay, so you're a long way from home."

"Yes sir, but I won't be here long. I see you have my son with you."

"He said he came here looking for you."

Daniel nodded. "Good. I'm glad to see him here."

"All right, let me talk to someone who lives here. If there are no complaints, I'll be on my way." The officer talked with Marie in the doorway.

Colton stepped toward Daniel. "Are you alright?"

Daniel nodded again."

"Mom was frantic. You weren't after some guy like we talked before?"

"No, no. But–" Daniel took a deep breath." They

know about that back at the station. I'm going back. I have to go back."

"So why are you here?" Colton's expression remained concerned, but his tone wanted answers.

"That young lady there will give us a ride. You'll get answers to all your questions."

When the Spinler police officer left, Marie opened the garage door remotely.

Colton stepped forward and smiled. "I'm Colton. Thanks for giving us a ride."

Marie looked at him as though he were a rock star. "No problem," she said, as her brain did a visual double take and she turned back toward the garage.

Daniel rode in the front seat while Marie drove.

"Are we going back to the motel," Colton asked.

"No, we're making a stop at the cemetery so I can pay respects to an old friend."

Marie pulled into the parking area. They walked over cobblestone paths across a wooden bridge to an area of new graves beside a gently spewing fountain. The berm over Margie's grave was still covered with green outdoor carpet, but the headstone had already been placed. It read:

Margaret Nell Rucker

June 25, 1971 — October 30, 2010

Daniel sat on the carpet and bowed his head and cried. The youngsters found a nearby bench and sat together.

"Who is that?" Colton asked.

"That's my mother. She died last week."

"I'm so sorry to hear that."

"She was pretty much my best friend, but I did

all my crying at the funeral. She was his sweetheart in college. I guess he never got over her. I know she never got over him.

"Really? But she got married."

Marie could only shrug her shoulders. "He broke into the house while I was still in my room."

"Oh no. I'm so sorry.

"Scared me to death at first but when I told him my mother had died, I could tell he was as sad as I was."

Colton looked up at the sky. "So that's why he came here–to see your mother."

"Yes, I'd say so." Both of them watched as Daniel knelt beside the marker and traced every word on the headstone with his finger.

Colton looked at her more closely. "Can I ask you how old you are?"

Marie gave a sheepish smile, "I'll be nineteen in the spring."

"So you're in college?"

"Senior year in high school."

Colton gazed into her shimmering blue eyes. Would you like to go out with me sometime?"

For a moment, Marie lost the ability to speak. But she quickly recovered and delivered the best retort that popped in her brain. "Well, I might like to, but I don't usually date older men."

Colton's jaw dropped, but then he smiled. "Wow, you know how to hurt a guy. How old do you think I am?"

"Oh, I'd say around thirty."

"You don't mean that." He stopped and looked at the young woman beside him. "How can someone so pretty be so clever?"

Her eyes were aglow with mischief and she cocked her head in a cute little tilt.

"Okay, I say you're twenty-five."

"I won't be twenty-four until January."

"Well then, I guess I could make an exception."

"Is there anything to do around here?" Colton asked.

"Not unless you want to bowl."

"Not for me. I'll tell you what. Next Saturday, I'll be at your house at 4 p.m. We could go to Austin and catch all the fanfare on 6th Avenue."

"Oh, I'd love that," she said.

"But I'll need one thing before I go, if you don't mind?"

"What?" She sounded truly confused.

"Do you have a name?"

"Oh, of course. I'm Marie."

Colton leaned toward her just a bit. "I don't even know you, but I already like you."

Marie dropped her gaze and paused. "Thank you. I like you, too. But we better get your father somewhere he can rest and get his mind off that headstone."

Colton and Marie went to Daniel and literally pulled him to a standing position and escorted him back to the car.

CHAPTER THIRTY-NINE

After a night's sleep, Daniel and Colton each drove their cars back to Dallas. Brenda and the girls were happy. Daniel was back home. However, his legal troubles had only begun. His unexcused absence from work, not to mention the line-up, got him fired from the police force. When eyewitnesses came forward, he was charged with multiple counts of assault and battery. The Dallas DA's office went lenient on him because no one was killed, seriously injured, or robbed. Still, Daniel was sentenced to 3 to 5 years in the state penitentiary.

Because he was an ex-cop, Daniel was placed in segregated housing. With good behavior, he could be out in a year. Thoughts of Margie quit being feelings of longing, replaced by nothing but sadness. The pain of her passing was great, but he fought off the memories. When he got out, he'd take Brenda by the hand and renew their vows.

But there were others who knew Daniel King had been fired as a cop and was currently in the pen. Bruce Keck and Heath Diebold were counting the days until his release.

But the word revenge didn't come close to the blinding hate that now consumed Robert Rucker. While storing Margie's things and checking drawers, Robert came across a worn notebook. On almost every page were personal letters written by his wife. Robert read a few and steam boiled from his ears. He knew what the capital M and D meant. He was beyond furious. This man was the cause of his wife's death. If he could kill the man with a high-powered rifle shot from 300 yards, he would. But what he really wanted was to make the man suffer. Robert Rucker would know the date of King's release and would stalk the man from that day on until he found a chance to kill him.

the saga continues with
Colton's Crossroads
release date December 1st